THE SAINT TO
THE RESCUE

LESLIE CHARTERIS

These are the titles in order of sequence
(the original titles are shown in brackets)

LESLIE CHARTERIS

THE SAINT TO
THE RESCUE

HODDER PAPERBACKS

Copyright © 1956, 1957, 1958, 1959
by Leslie Charteris
FIRST PUBLISHED   OCTOBER 1961
HODDER PAPERBACK EDITION 1963
SECOND IMPRESSION   1965
THIRD IMPRESSION   1970

Printed and bound in Great Britain for
Hodder Paperbacks Ltd.,
St. Paul's House, Warwick Lane,
London, E.C.4
by Hazell Watson & Viney Ltd.,
Aylesbury, Bucks

SBN 340 01729 5

CONTENTS

The Ever-Loving Spouse

THE Saint met Otis Q Fennick on the fire escape of the Hotel Mercurio, San Francisco, at about four o'clock in the morning.

Like many another eminently simple statement, the foregoing now involves an entirely disproportionate series of explanations.

Simon Templar was staying at the Mercurio, which was a long way from attaining the luxurious standards of the kind of hotel that he usually frequented, because when he headed for San Francisco he had neglected to inform himself that a national convention of the soft-drink and candy industry was concurrently infesting that otherwise delightful city. After finding every superior hostelry clogged to the rafters with manufacturers and purveyors of excess calories, he had decided that he was lucky to find a room in any hotel at all.

The room itself was one of the least desirable even under that second-rate roof, being situated at the back of the building overlooking a picturesque alley tastefully bordered with garbage cans and directly facing an eye-filling panorama of grimy windows and still grimier walls appertaining to the edifice across the way. The iron steps of the outside fire escape partly obscured this appealing view by slanting across the upper half of the window; and it was there that Simon first heard the stealthy feet of Mr Fennick, and a moment later, being of a curious disposition, saw them through a gap at the edge of the ill-fitting blind. He had dined at his friend Johnny Kan's temple of oriental gastronomy on Grant Avenue for old times' sake, and afterwards Johnny had insisted that they should go out together and look for some late entertainment that might not have been discovered by the assembled exploiters of appetizing toothache, and what with one thing and another it had been very late when he got home, and he had only just shed most of his clothes and brushed his teeth when he heard the furtive scuffling outside which was the surreptitious descent of Mr Fennick.

In such a situation, the ordinary sojourner in even a second-rate hotel would either have remained gawking in numb perplexity or have started howling an alarum, with or without the intermediacy of the house phone. Not being ordinary in any way, Simon Templar rolled up the shade with a craftsman's touch which almost miraculously silenced its antique mechanism—he had already switched off the lights in order to see out better, and the window had never been closed since he accepted the room, on account of the stuffiness of its location—and swung himself across to the nearest landing of the fire escape with the deceptively effortless grace of a trained gymnast, having reacted with such dazzling speed that he arrived there simultaneously with the cautiously groping prowler.

"Me Tarzan," said the Saint seductively. "You Jane?"

His voice should not have been at all terrifying—in fact, it was carefully pitched low enough to have been inaudible to anyone who had not already been disturbed by Mr Fennick's rather clumsy creeping. But Mr Fennick was apparently unused to being accosted on fire escapes, or perhaps even to being on them at all; at any rate, it was immediately obvious that no intelligible sound was going to emerge for a while from the fish-like opening of his mouth. It became clear to Simon that the acquaintance would have to be developed in a more leisurely manner and less unconventional surroundings.

8

"You'd better come in before you catch cold or break your neck," he said.

Mr Fennick gave him no struggle. He was a small man, and the Saint's steel fingers almost met their thumb around the upper arm that they had persuasively clamped on. He squeezed his eyes very tightly shut, like a little boy, as Simon half lifted him across the space to the window sill, which was really no more than a long stride except for having about forty feet of empty air under it.

With the blind drawn and the lights on again, the Saint inspected his catch with proprietary interest. Mr Fennick wore a well-pressed brown double-breasted suit of conservative tailoring, a white stiff-collared shirt, a tie very modestly patterned with neutral greens, and even a clean felt hat of sedate contour. To match his skinny frame, he had a rather wizened face with a sharp thin nose, a wide thin mouth, and lively intelligent brown eyes when he opened them. He looked much more like a member of some Chamber of Commerce and pillar of the Community Church than a felonious skulker on fire escapes.

"You know," said the Saint at last, "I don't think you're a burglar after all. And this would be a rather desperate hour for a Peeping Tom. I guess you must be a candy cooker."

"That's right," Mr Fennick said eagerly. "The Fennick Candy Company. You must have heard of it."

He whipped out a wallet and extracted a card from it with an automatic dexterity which even his temporarily shattered condition could not radically unhinge. He went on, in a kind of delirious incantation: "Jumbo Juices, Crunchy Wunchies, Crackpops, Yummigum——"

"That sounds like a powerful spell," said the Saint respectfully. "Now are you supposed to vanish in a puff of smoke, or am I?"

9

"I wish I could," said Mr Otis Q Fennick, President, forlornly.

Having read everything on the card, Simon put it down on the dresser and picked up a cigarette.

"It begins to seem as if you have a problem," he said. "But presumably it isn't anything so sordid as not being able to pay your bill. You weren't doing the moonlight flit, were you?"

"Oh, dear me, no! I'm quite comfortably well off, I assure you. In fact, I was most upset with the convention Committee for booking me into a place like this. Of course, they said that all the rooms were allotted by drawing names out of a hat, but I noticed that they all got the Mark Hopkins or the Drake. This isn't at all the class of hotel I'd choose for myself."

"We have that in common, anyhow."

"I don't remember seeing you at any of the meetings. What's your line?"

"I was referring to our taste in hotels, Otis. I've never taken much interest in candy, unless it happened to be poisoned."

"Oh." Mr Fennick looked pardonably vague. "Well, I am attending this soft-drink and candy convention which you may have heard of——"

"I could hardly help it. It stuck me with this dump—and me not even a delegate. So what were you doing just now? Trying to sneak in on one of your competitors and steal his secret formula for the ultimate frightful blend of peppermint, popcorn, and peanut butter, with the miracle self-inflating ingredient and the atomic crackle?"

"No, nothing like that——"

"Then it must have been his new sales gimmick to top your offer of a rocket trip to Venus in exchange for fifty million Crunchy Wunchy wrappers."

Mr Fennick blinked at him.

"You must be misinformed, sir. The Fennick Candy Company never made any such offer."

"Then I'll make you a present of the idea. So what *were* you doing?"

"Well, I suppose I was just in a panic. I knew I was being framed."

"Maybe you were," said the Saint cheerfully. "But I still don't get the picture. Why don't you begin at the beginning?"

Mr Fennick gulped, wriggled miserably, and took a deep breath like a diver about to plunge.

"All right. I was out last night—it would be last night, wouldn't it? I was out with some business connections. We had dinner at the Sheraton Palace, and went to some night clubs. We were at the Forbidden City, and Bimbo's. Of course, we drank quite a lot——"

"Coke, or chemical fruit punch?"

"No, I like a real drink when I go out. But I wasn't drunk. You must believe me. I only mentioned it to explain why I must have fallen asleep especially soundly when I got to bed, which was about two o'clock."

"Why must you?"

"Because when I woke up, there was this girl in bed with me, with nothing on. And I hadn't heard her come in, or get undressed, or anything."

The Saint's blue eyes became slightly wider.

"Wow! . . . I mean, that must have been disappointing. You probably missed the best strip-tease of the evening."

"I give you my word, sir, I'm not used to anything like that. At least, not at such close quarters."

"Don't be discouraged, chum. It may grow on you yet. The *savoir faire* comes with practice. What did you do—offer her some Yummigum?"

"I think I woke up when the lights suddenly went on. Or when she leaned over and put her arms around me.

Both things seemed to happen together. I was completely fuddled, of course. And then, before I could really get my bearings at all, the light blinded me. I think there was someone else in the room, but I was too dazzled to have anything more than an impression. And then, something hit me on the head, and it hurt terribly, and everything went black. It all seems like a bad dream now, except . . ."

The little man took off his prim felt hat and gingerly touched the upper side of his cranium. The mousy hair had ebbed far enough from that region for the Saint without even coming closer to authenticate a swelling that was already making its first experiments with the palette of colour effects.

"What happened when you woke up again?" Simon asked.

"There wasn't anyone there. Except me, of course. And as soon as I could think it out, I knew I'd been framed. That blinding light—obviously, a flash bulb. Somebody had taken a picture of me, in that *awful* situation."

"Was this doll really gruesome?"

"No. No, not at all. That's what makes it so dreadful. In fact, she was . . . well, er——"

"Stacked?"

Mr Fennick winced, his pallor taking on a definite tint of rose.

"I don't particularly like such vulgar expressions. But, yes, if someone was planning to blackmail me, I suppose she'd be the type they'd use."

"Then all may not be lost," said the Saint consolingly. "If some prankster in this Convention is trying to sabotage your bid to be elected Supreme Lollipop by charging you with dissolute habits, the foul conspiracy may yet boomerang. With your new reputation as the Confectionery Casanova, you might become the hero of the Convention. Think what a few shots like that did for Brigitte Bardot."

"I am hardly in the same category," said Mr Fennick severely. "And in my case, that'd be all my wife would need."

Simon Templar nodded.

"Aha. Now it starts to make sense. I gather that Mrs Fennick isn't here with you."

"No, she's home in New York."

"Enjoying The Theatre, The Ballet, and The Mink, no doubt."

"Yes, she likes all those things. And she thinks conventions are just an excuse for a lot of men to cut loose and—well, you know. . . ."

"Get into the sort of mischief you were photographed in?"

"Exactly."

"So that if you tried to explain that snapshot the way you've told it to me, you'd expect a fairly hilarious reception."

"I wouldn't have the least chance of convincing her."

"I see." The Saint produced a thoughtful aureole of smoke. "But at the risk of seeming to harp on the subject, chum, I'm still trying to find out why you were cavorting on the fire escape."

Mr Fennick wrung his hands—it was the first time Simon had seen that well-worn cliché actually performed, and it corrected his lifelong delusion that it was merely a slightly archaic figure of speech.

"As I told you, I went into a funk. The only thing I could think of was to find the young woman and try to persuade her that whatever she'd been paid for playing her part, I could make it a little more worth her while to testify to the truth."

"Because that'd certainly be less than half what the photographer or *his* boss would be expecting to collect. Not bad thinking, for a guy who just came out of a conk on the noggin. But what made you think she'd be hanging on the wall outside?"

"Nothing. But I had an idea where to begin looking."

The Saint's eyes narrowed fractionally.

"So you did know her, after all."

"I had seen her once before," Mr Fennick said precisely. "As a matter of fact, that's what made it seem so specially shocking and like a dream when I woke up and saw her without—um—the way I described her. She works in the bar downstairs, in the hotel, with one of the flashlight cameras, getting customers to have souvenir pictures taken."

"Then why didn't you go down in the elevator, like any respectably indignant customer, and start yelling for the manager?"

"Because I felt certain that somebody on the staff must have been in on the plot. I'm always very careful about locking my door in hotels. Somebody must have given those people a key, or let them into my room. It might have been the elevator boy, or the night clerk——"

"Why couldn't they have used the fire escape, too?"

"My window was only open a few inches, and there's a safety chain on the inside. I expect yours has one, too, because of the fire escape being so close. I remembered to make sure the chain was fastened before I went to bed—I don't carry an excessive amount of cash with me, but I don't believe in taking unnecessary chances. . . . Well, I thought, if any of the other accomplices sees me looking for the girl, they'll know I recognized her, and they'd do anything to keep us apart."

"Didn't you think anyone would see you talking to her in the bar?"

"That's why I had to take such extreme steps to avoid the lobby. I intended to wait outside, hoping to follow her when she went home."

Simon regarded Mr Fennick with increasing respect. It was becoming indisputably manifest that in spite of his somewhat dehydrated aspect, prissy personality, and fluttering agitation, this bonbon baron had something more active than nougat in his noodle.

"I couldn't have figured it any better myself if I'd had all the facts," he murmured, picking up his recently discarded shirt and sliding an idle arm into a sleeve. "But by the same logic, Otis, old bean, I think this is where I'll have to take over."

The little man stared.

"You?"

"There's nothing wrong with your analysis except that it stops short. Never mind about being seen talking to this chick—you can't even afford to let *her* hear you. Suppose she doesn't go for your bid, which could happen for a whole flock of reasons. You'd only have told the Ungodly how scared they've got you, and bang goes any chance of bluffing them out of a showdown. Whereas someone else could move in as your representative, proving you're not all alone in the world, and talking tough, and maybe give 'em some worries they weren't expecting."

Mr Fennick pursed his lips, with commendable acuteness for a man in his disconcerting predicament.

"Quite possibly; but why should you, Mr——"

"Templar. Simon Templar."

In those later days of the Saint's career, it was no longer such a potentially interesting moment when he gave his real name to a stranger for the first time. The range of possible reactions had become rather standardized. Still, there was always the hope of evoking some absolutely novel response.

Mr Fennick inclined his head with mechanical politeness.

"—Mr Templar," he continued, with hardly a break. "I've already imposed on you enough——"

"But I insist," said the Saint genially. "And if you give me any trouble, I might have to call the house detective, if this roach farm has such a person, and turn you in as a captured burglar."

He had tucked in his shirt tails and almost absent-mindedly knotted a tie while this part of the conversation went on; and now by simply shrugging into a coat he was suddenly so completely dressed and ready for any eventuality that his uninvited guest could only open and shut his mouth ineffectually.

"Don't go away, Otis," he said from the door. "Just in case your pals haven't run out of cute tricks, or in case we might have to pull some quaint switch of our own, it might be clever not to give anyone a chance to prove you've been in your room lately. Who knows—we might even dare them to prove that that picture wasn't taken years before you got married, or even that it's your picture at all. Anyhow, wait till I bring you the first bulletin."

He was gone before he could be delayed by any further argument.

The elevator was piloted by the same jockey who had taken him up only a little while ago, an elderly individual with drooping shoulders and an air of comatose resignation to the infinite monotony of endlessly identical vertical voyages. He revealed no curiosity or interest whatsoever in why the Saint should want to ride down again at such an hour: one felt that he had long since been anesthetized against anything that could happen in a hotel during a convention, and perhaps at any other time.

"Tell me," said the Saint, with elaborately casual candour. "If I wanted to play a joke on one of the fellows— a friend of mine— could you let me into his room?"

The man did not even turn his head. In fact, for a

number of seconds he appeared to have been afflicted with deafness, until at the ultimate limit of plausible cogitation he wrung from himself a single word of decision:

"Depends."

"On what?"

The instant the words were out of his mouth, Simon knew he had been too fast. The man pointedly made him wait even longer for the next reply, as a form of corrective discipline.

"Plenty."

The lift shuddered to a stop at the ground floor, and the gate rumbled open. The pilot held it, waiting for the Saint to disembark, with such a total lack of eagerness to pursue the conversation that except for his minimal movements it would have been easy to believe that he was stuffed.

Simon got out, and followed the direction of a neon arrow which proclaimed that it pointed to The Rowdy Room. This proved to be a depressingly under-lighted cavern decorated in blood red and funeral black, with a dance floor large enough for a minuet by four midgets and an orchestra alcove furnished with an upright piano and stands for two other instrumentalists, all of whom had obviously racked up all the overtime they wanted and called it a day. The only rowdiness left was being provided by a quartet of die-hards in one corner, two of whom were foggily listening to some obscure argument being loudly elaborated by the third, while the fourth was frankly falling asleep. The bartender, listlessly polishing glasses, accepted the Saint's arrival with a disinterested stare which barely suggested that if Simon wanted anything he could ask for it.

Simon ordered a Peter Dawson on the rocks, and after he had tasted it, he said: "Where's the gal who takes the pictures?"

"Norma? She ain't here."

"That settles one thing," said the Saint mildly. "I was wondering if she'd become invisible."

The barman squinted at him suspiciously, and said: "She went home early. Had a headache or sump'n."

"Would you know where I can get in touch with her?"

"She'll be here tomorrow."

"That's the trouble—I may be leaving in the afternoon, much earlier than she'd come to work. I wanted to see her about some pictures that were taken the other night."

"Well, whyncha say so?" demanded the bartender aggrievedly.

He fumbled through some litter beside the cash register, and turned back with a card. The ornate printing on it could be reduced to VERE BALTON, *Photography*, and an address, 685 Scoden Street.

"I thought you called her Norma," Simon said.

"I did. Balton is the guy who has the concession. She works for him."

"Where is Scoden Street?"

"About five-six blocks from here, on the left off of Geary."

"And what's her name?"

"I tolja, Norma," said the other, with obviously increasing impatience with so much stupidity.

"Nothing else?"

"You tell 'em Norma took the pitchers here," said the bartender. "They'll take care of ya."

"Thank you," said the Saint.

He finished his drink, put down the exact price and a minimum tip, and sauntered back to the lobby.

If the shapely Norma was not averse to providing certain extracurricular services of the type indicated by Mr Fennick's story, it was highly implausible that the bartender would know nothing about it. Indeed, it was most probable that he would sometimes help to procure them.

Therefore the Saint couldn't insist on getting in touch with her too urgently, or pressing the questioning too hard, without the risk of telegraphing a warning to the quarry he had yet to identify.

Behind the reception desk, the night clerk, a weedy young man with long hair and acne, was totting up stacks of vouchers on an adding machine. He kept Simon waiting while he clicked his way stubbornly through to the end of a pile, and then looked up with an unctuous affectation of attentiveness.

"Yes, sir?"

"I'm afraid I left my key upstairs," said the Saint. "Can you let me have a spare? Room four-o-nine."

"What is the name, sir?"

"Templar."

The clerk ducked aside behind a screen that blocked one end of the counter, but he could be heard flipping the pages of an index. After some further groping in a drawer he bobbed back, holding a key.

"Could you show me anything with your name on it, sir?"

Simon impassively produced a driver's licence, and the clerk handed over the key.

"Do you put everyone through this when they lock themselves out?" Simon inquired mildly.

"Yes, sir, if I don't know them. You can't be too careful, at this hour of the night, I always say. Especially during a convention."

"Why especially during a convention?"

"When they get too full of the spirit of the thing, sir, delegates often think of practical jokes to play on each other—all in good fun, of course, but not always appreciated by the victim. You yourself, sir, mightn't be amused if you found a live seal in your bathtub, and found out that my negligence had enabled your friends to plant it there."

"I guess you have a point."

The pimply one bared his yellow teeth ingratiatingly.

"I knew you'd see it, sir. Thank you. Goodnight, sir," he said, and picked up another sheaf of checks and resumed the busy tapping of his calculator keys without another upward glance.

Simon stepped into the elevator, and the lugubrious liftman let go a carpet sweeper which he was pushing lethargically about the foyer and started the ascent in stoic silence.

Finally the Saint asked : "Plenty of what?"

After another floor had gone by, it transpired that the driver had not lost the thread of his lucubrations.

"Things," he opined darkly.

They were at the fourth floor again. He held the gate open, without looking at the Saint, but with a rugged air of self-satisfaction with his achievements in both navigation and diplomacy. Simon got out, and headed back to his room.

His excursion had yielded nothing sensational, but at least he had half a name, an address which might be the start of a trail, and some observations which might interest Mr Fennick.

The trouble was that Otis Q Fennick was not there to hear about them.

The room was not big enough to hide even such a slight man as Mr Fennick anywhere except in the closet or under the bed. But if he had been even more jittery than he had shamelessly confessed, it was remotely possible that he could be terrified of anyone who might enter.

"Otis, old marshmallow," said the Saint reassuringly. "It's only me—Templar."

There was no answer.

The bathroom door was ajar. Simon looked inside. Mr Fennick was not there. Nor was he in the closet, or under the bed—Simon ultimately forced himself to verify both places, foolish though it made him feel. But in about half the detective stories that the Saint had read, one of those locations could have been practically counted on to reveal Mr Fennick's freshly perforated corpse. None of them did. It was almost disappointing.

Simon went to the dresser for the pack of cigarettes which he had left where he put down Mr Fennick's business card. Now he found the card tucked half into the opening of the package, in such a way that he couldn't have extracted a cigarette without having his attention focused on it. On the back had been written, in a cramped but meticulous script :

> *I simply can't let you bother with my*
> *problems. I'll just have to pay up and*
> *make the best of it. Please forget the*
> *whole thing.*

Simon sat down on the bed and picked up the telephone.

"Mr Fennick, please," he said.

"One moment, sir." It was the oleaginous voice of the night clerk, who was evidently entrusted with several chores by a thrifty management. Then : "I'm sorry, sir, but Mr Fennick's line still has a Do Not Disturb on it."

"Since when ?"

"He asked me to put it on when he came in, sir, at one-thirty."

"I see. . . . Would you give me his room number ?"

The pause this time was almost imperceptible.

"I'm afraid I couldn't take the responsibility for that,

sir. He might be very annoyed if you disturbed him by knocking on his door."

"What makes you think I'd do that?"

"I'm sure you wouldn't want to, sir. So you won't mind asking the manager for the information, will you? He comes on at eight o'clock. Thank you, sir."

"Invite me to your funeral," said the Saint sweetly, but he said it after a click in the receiver had announced that the clerk had already terminated the discussion.

For a few minutes, in a simmer of sheer exasperation, he contemplated some quite extravagant forms of retaliation against everyone who had contributed to wasting his time for the past hour. But at the end of a cigarette he laughed, and fell asleep thinking it was lucky he hadn't gone any farther on a wild-goose chase with such a protégé.

If Mr Otis Q Fennick was such an eviscerated marvel that he insisted on submitting to the crudest kind of contrived shakedown, without even a struggle, after having been offered the best advice and assistance, then he deserved to stew in his own syrup.

The Saint slumbered on this relaxing justification for precisely three hours and seventeen minutes, at which time a crew of civic servants arrived under his window with some raspingly geared conveyance and began to decant into it the garbage cans which had previously been only silent ornaments of the alley, clanging and crashing them back and forth as a tympanic accompaniment to their mutual shouts of encouragement and impromptu snatches of vocalizing.

By the time they had moved on he was wide awake and knew that he had no hope of feeling drowsy again that morning. But as he lay still stretched out with his eyes closed the entire Fennick episode unrolled again in his memory, and the earlier mood of exasperation crept back.

Only instead of being a petulant flash of anger, it was now a considered and solid resentment that could not be dismissed.

He tried to dismiss it while he got up and showered and shaved and went down to the coffee shop for breakfast, but it refused to go away.

"You've got every excuse to duck this," he had to tell himself finally, "except one that'll let you forget it."

If Mr Fennick consented to pay blackmail, it could well be maintained that that was Mr Fennick's own private business, and the hell with him. But if a blackmailer got away with blackmail, that had always been the Saint's self-appointed business, as had any kind of unpunished evil. And it was doubly so when the circumstances ruled out any possibility of legal retribution.

Simon finished his second cup of coffee and went back through the lobby, where a totally different staff had taken over. This time he had no difficulty in getting Mr Fennick's room number, which was 607; but the switchboard operator told him that the Do Not Disturb was still on the phone. For a moment he contemplated going up and banging on the door; but then he reflected that Mr Fennick, in the shattered condition in which the sweetmeat sachem must have regained his room, had probably taken a sleeping pill and would not exactly scintillate if he were prematurely aroused.

Meanwhile, the Saint had in his pocket the card which the un-cooperative bartender had given him. It might not be much, but it was something. And at least it might help to pass the time constructively.

Scoden Street was a narrow turning off one of the drabber stretches of Geary, given over to a few small dispirited neighbourhood shops jumbled among other nondescript buildings of which some had been converted into the dingier type of offices and some still offered lodgings of dubious desirability. Number 685 seemed to combine the two latter types, for a window on the street level was lettered with the words VERE BALTON STUDIOS on the glass, behind which an assortment of arty enlargements were attached to a velvet backdrop, while on the entrance door was tacked a large printed card with the legend APARTMENT FOR RENT.

The door was open, though only a couple of inches.

Simon pushed it with his toe and went in.

He found himself in a small dark hallway, at the rear of which a flight of worn wooden stairs started upwards, doubtless to the vacant apartment. Immediately on his right was a door, also ajar, with a shingle projecting from the lintel on which the VERE BALTON STUDIOS sign was repeated. He went through into a sort of reception room formed by the space between the shoulder-height backdrop of the front window and a set of full-length drapes which shut off the rest of the premises. It contained a shabby desk and three equally shabby chairs, but none of them was occupied.

"Hi," said the Saint, raising his voice. "Anybody home?"

There was no reply, or even any sound of movement. But the long drapes were not fully drawn, and through the aperture he could see a yellowness of artificial light.

He went to the opening and looked into a small studio equipped with a dais, a tripod camera, and the usual clutter of lamps, screens, and props to sit on or lean against. But nobody was utilizing the props, and the only lamp alight was a bare bulb hanging from the ceiling.

Simon stepped on through the curtains. The near corner inside had been partitioned off with Beaverboard into a cubicle which from the sinks and shelves of bottles that could be seen through its wide open door was obviously used as a darkroom; but no one was using it. At the opposite end of the studio was another door, half open.

"Anybody home?" Simon repeated.

Nobody acknowledged it.

He crossed the studio quietly, cutting a zigzag course between the paraphernalia, and his second tack put him at an angle from which he could see the body that lay on the floor of the back room.

It belonged to a fat man of medium height with dirty grey hair and a rather porcine face to which death had not added any dignity. There were three bullet holes in the front of his patchily reddened white shirt, loosely grouped around the *VB* monogram placed like a target over his heart, and two of them were ringed with the powder burn and stain of almost contact range.

Simon bent and touched the back of his hand to one of the flabby cheeks—not to verify the fact of death, which was unnecessary, but to determine if it was very recent. The skin was cold.

The room was an office, furnished with an antique roll-top desk, a hardly less antique typewriter, and a bank of unmatched filing cabinets. Nude colour-calendar photos were pinned up on much of the wall space, interspersed with glossy monochromes of similar esthetic subjects. The desk was littered with a hodgepodge of correspondence, bills, prints, and negatives; and about half the filing drawers were open to varying extents, many of them with folders partly raised out of them. Nevertheless, the general impression, strengthened by the film of dust that could be observed on many surfaces, was not so much that of a recent ransacking as of an ancient and incurable disorder.

But why should there have been any ransacking? With his rolled-up sleeves and his coat over the back of a chair, Vere Balton hadn't surprised any intruder—he had been surprised. And with a gun in his chest, he would have been glad to produce whatever the intruder wanted in exchange for his life, hoping he would not be cheated. . . .

All this went through the Saint's mind in a consecutive rush, like a cascade through a sieve. But before it had finished draining through, one scrap of flotsam was caught.

Mr Otis Q Fennick was entangled, consciously or not, with something bigger than a candid shot of himself in the hay with a buxom brunette whose name was not on his marriage licence.

Simon backed out of the office on tiptoe, and retraced his steps even more circumspectly between the obstacles and over the coiling cables of the studio lights, being careful to leave no clumsy traces of his visit. But in the anteroom in front he stopped by the desk on which he had seen the telephone. That was the logical place to look for one item of information that he had come for, and he found it in the first drawer he opened with a handkerchief wrapped around his fingers. There was an address book, precisely where one would expect it to be kept, and he turned the pages with the same precaution against leaving fingerprints, scanning each one swiftly but completely.

He had to go nearly all the way through the book before he came to a Norma, and not much farther to be positive that there were no others. He turned back and memorized the entry with a second glance:

> *Norma Uplitz*
> *5 De Boer Lane—Apt. 2*
> *AG 2-9044*

Not the most likely name for the sexily constructed siren that Mr Fennick had indicated, but a lot of Hollywood queens had started life even less glamorously baptized.

He had not touched either of the entrance doors with his hands when he came in, he recalled, and he went out without touching them. He did pull the front door almost shut, before he put his handkerchief away, leaving it as nearly as possible in the same position as he had found it. Let the police have the benefit of any clues that might be latent in the set-up: the Saint's only concern was not to interpolate any new ones which might point misleadingly to himself.

The greatest risk seemed to be that someone might remember seeing him going in or coming out. That was a hazard which he shared with the real killer. But the ultimate danger to himself was much less, for if that hypothetical witness took any note of the time, it would prove that the Saint had been there several hours after the autopsy would show that Vere Balton had died. So he took his departure boldly and unhurriedly, making no special effort to avoid being observed—which was perhaps the best of all guarantees against being noticed.

He walked back to the Mercurio and took the elevator directly to the sixth floor, without wasting any time on the house phone. He did not have to hesitate over the route to Room 607, for the number told him it must be next door to the same relative location as his own door.

There was no Do Not Disturb card hung on the door knob, but it would not have moderated his peremptory knock if there had been.

The door opened almost instantly; and for one of the few times in his life Simon Templar felt that only the sang-froid of a sphinx saved him from falling over backwards.

It was not Otis Q Fennick who opened the door. It was

a blonde. And no part of her configuration remotely resembled that of the creator of Crackpots.

It was, however, strikingly reminiscent of the general impression that Mr Fennick had haltingly conveyed of his unauthorized cot companion. But one specification that Simon was unshakably clear about was that Mr Fennick's surprise package had been distinctly described as a brunette.

This blonde had not been manufactured in the past few hours. She might have owed something to tints and rinses, but the foundation was genetic. The Saint could tell. And as other minutiae gradually registered on him, they declined unanimously to fit into the reconstruction of a frill who hustled photos in a joint like the Rowdy Room and would blow more than a flash bulb for a fast bill. This one's dress had the unmistakable cachet of expensive exclusiveness, and any one of the small ornaments she wore would have outvalued Norma Uplitz's whole treasure chest of jewels. This one might be available too, for the right proposition, but the price tag would be liable to sift the boys by their tax brackets.

"I beg your pardon," said the Saint, with a sensation of laboriously cranking his chin up off his necktie. "I was looking for Mr Fennick."

"He isn't here."

"But this is his room?"

"Yes. He just happens to be out."

"Oh."

"It's perfectly respectable," said the blonde. "I'm his wife."

"His . . ."

"Wife. You must have heard the expression. Are you feeling all right? You look rather glassy-eyed."

Simon strove valiantly to unglaze. It required an abnormal effort, but the multiplication of shocks was proceeding a trifle rapidly even for him. And the day had scarcely begun.

"I was a bit startled," he admitted. "I understood you were in New York."

"I was—yesterday. But these new jets are so sudden. Do you have some business with him, or are you a friend?"

"To tell you the truth, I only met him last night. But we became quite chummy."

"I can imagine it. Do you sell candy, or is it soda pop?"

"Neither. We just happened to be at the same hotel, and we bumped into each other. One of those things."

"I thought you looked different from most of his business buddies. Come in."

Simon had intended to from the moment he saw her. The room was virtually a facsimile of his own, and the blonde looked as out of place in it as a piece of Cartier hardware in a junk yard. But the observation he wanted to make was that Mr Fennick really wasn't there. The closet was open, and he was able to check under the bed by clumsily dropping the pack of cigarettes he slipped out of his pocket.

"As a matter of fact, you might be able to help me to catch up with him," said the blonde. "I only arrived late last night myself—it was all on the spur of the moment, and I didn't even try to call him till this morning. I know what these conventions are like. I spent the night with an old girl friend who lives here."

"I was wondering how you got in. That's why I looked so dazed when I saw you."

"They gave me a key at the desk, of course, as soon as I proved I was Mrs Fennick. Why shouldn't they?"

"I called him less than an hour ago," said the Saint, "and his phone was still shut off."

"It was shut off when I called from downstairs ten

minutes ago. So I came on up anyhow. Exercising a marital privilege. I didn't see why I should have to sit in the lobby till he condescended to regain consciousness. But no Otis."

"He must have gone out and forgotten to clear the line."

"Do you solve crossword puzzles, too?"

Simon had been opening his cigarette package, which was a fresh one, with unhurried neatness. He offered her the first of its contents, which she accepted.

"I can't solve any puzzle about where he may have gone," he said, striking a match. "He didn't tell me anything about his plans for the day."

"May I ask why you thought he wouldn't mind your waking him up, if he was trying to sleep late?"

"I happened to have dug up a hot lead on something he was telling me he was very concerned about financially. I thought he ought to know it at once, so I took a chance."

On the pretext of looking for a safe place to get rid of the match, he contrived to work himself around to a sufficient glimpse of the bathroom to confirm that Mr Fennick was not hiding out there, or stashed there as a corpse. He was aware that he might begin to seem obsessed by such possibilities, but he could certainly have offered a doozy of an excuse.

"Well," she said, "that seems to leave us both in the same boat. He's probably lost for the day now. They have meetings and lunches and speeches and more meetings, from the first hangover till it's time to start the next one, don't they, on these conventions?"

"I wouldn't know," Simon grinned. "I've never been part of one."

"Ah, yes. I said that you didn't look like the type."

"Neither do you, Mrs Fennick."

She had been studying him with unmistakably increasing interest for the last few minutes, and her appraising eyes did not waver by a fraction of a degree at the intangible hint of audacity in his tone.

She said : "Did you get chummy enough, as you put it, to call my husband Otis?"

"I guess I did."

"Then you needn't be so formal with me. If he didn't tell you, the name is Liane. Do you have a name, too? Or a number?"

"Simon Templar."

"The Saint, of course. All right, I can enjoy a joke. But eventually you'll have to explain why it's funny. And what type don't I look like?"

"The wife of a marzipan magnate," said the Saint, unabashed. "You look more like a glamour model."

"I was, not so many centuries ago. Lots of magnates pick up that type. Didn't you know? It adds prestige, like a Cadillac. Why don't we spend the day together, waiting for Otis, and I'll explain it all."

He would have had to be very much younger, very much older, or very much more naïve, to misunderstand the whole of her implication, and he let her know that he was weighing all of it in the long cool glance that he rested on her before he answered.

"It might be fun," he said, and he did not have to pretend to mean it. "But——"

"Don't tell me that Otis became your best friend overnight. And you don't look like a man who'd have any other objection to taking pity on a lady's boredom."

"He didn't, and I haven't. But I'd hate to help spoil a good thing for you."

"Did Otis give you the idea, in his cups, that we held hands every night while we made plans for our silver wedding honeymoon?"

"No. In fact, he gave me the impression that you were

the rolling-pin type, just waiting for him to come home with a smudge of lipstick under his ear. If you've got him as housebroken as that, it could be moderately catastrophic if he picked up the ammunition to shoot back at you."

"My good man, since we've suddenly become so very businesslike, let me remind you that the Fennicks are legal residents of the sovereign State of New York, which is also the legal domicile of the Fennick Candy Company. Have you ever heard any betting on a rich man's chances in a New York divorce court?"

"You sound as if you'd talked to some good lawyers."

She came so close, deliberately, that the first time they both inhaled simultaneously would have caused a most stimulating collision.

"Then why don't you let me worry about my own problems?"

He bent and carefully kissed her motionlessly upturned mouth. Then he stepped back and glanced at his watch.

He was not aware until afterwards of how cold-blooded he must have seemed. He didn't intend it as a rebuff. It was a long time since he had abjured any profound amazement at the strange impulses of women. Perhaps he had been exposed to too many of them. But in an oddly unegotistical way, for him, he was inclined to respect the privacy of their motives, and to enjoy the pleasant surprise without criticizing the donor. He had no moralistic resistance to Liane Fennick as an unexpected diversion, but there was a one-track quirk in his psychology that would not let him enjoy the best of it while he was still wound up with something else.

"There's another problem I've got to take care of," he said. "Let's make it a date for lunch."

She was palpably baffled by his restraint, but he couldn't help that. If he could have seen only a few hours into the future, he might have played it differently. But she took it well.

"Twelve-thirty?"

"I'll pick you up here."

"This time you'd better use the phone first," she said. "If it doesn't answer, or if Otis happens to have come back, I'll meet you at the Drake."

"But now," said the Saint regretfully, "I have got to duck."

He brushed her lips once more, with impudent promise, and went out.

An ingrained pattern of cautiousness that had become second nature made him walk down two flights of stairs before taking the elevator. It was not a question of exaggerated apprehensiveness, but a simple automatism of eliminating unnecessary risks. Whatever the intrusion of Liane Fennick might lead to, he could lose nothing by impressing the elevator boy with the fact that he rode down from his own floor, which would suffice to supplant any recollection of the floor he had gone up to.

The same habit made him ask the bell captain in the lobby for a street map of the city, instead of asking the whereabouts of De Boer Lane. There was no point in gratuitously enlarging the number of witnesses who might recall that he had inquired about that address.

And having located that short blind alley on one of the southern slopes of Telegraph Hill, he also picked out a convenient intersection three blocks away, and directed a taxi there, for the same good reason. From the intersection, after the taxi was out of sight, he walked. There was nothing prescient about it, except a logic which assumed that something had to be rotten in the state of Fennick. He didn't exhaust himself with trying to guess what it was. But after a very short stroll, he knew that his instincts had been impeccable at least on the score of procedure.

His taxi couldn't have reached De Boer Lane if he had begged it to. The street that it opened from was almost solid with police cars at that point, and an ambulance backed into the narrow turning blocked it completely. The lane was only about forty yards long, and was lined with small unmatched houses jammed shoulder to shoulder, none of them more than two stories high, the kind of cottages that lend themselves to cramped but quaint conversions and are therefore highly esteemed by would-be Bohemian types. It was the ideal backwater for a girl of Norma Uplitz's unconventional mores, where odd goings-on at odd hours would be so normal as to attract no attention. All except one aberration about which even the most sophisticated neighbourhoods are seldom blasé. . . .

The inevitable crowd of passers-by who had flowed in from the street was giving the native colony plenty of competition for the best view of the shrouded shape which at that moment was being carried out on a stretcher from a house halfway up the cul-de-sac.

The Saint did not need any parapsychic gifts to anticipate what the number of the building would be before he located it. And as he edged inconspicuously closer, he did not really need his exceptional visual acuity to decipher the name of Norma Uplitz on one of the mailboxes at the entrance. As for the infinitely ultimate possibility that the body on the stretcher could have come from the other of the two apartments, he had only to keep his ears open as he filtered through the morbid mob with the nearest approximation he could make to invisibility.

It was an alabaster-faced woman with mauve lipstick and stringy hair who said to a fellow colonist, an elderly bearded man with a gold earring : "Of course I heard the shots, dahling. How could I help it, living right underneath her? But I haven't the faintest idea what time it was, except that it was daylight. I only half woke up, and I thought she was probably slamming doors or hitting a paramour with a frying pan or some ordinary thing like that. I've had the most frightful job trying to explain to some yokel detective that I couldn't leap out of bed and start investigating every time there was an uproar in Norma's apartment. I'd never have got a good night's sleep...."

Simon drifted on, melting out of the crowd as self-effacingly as he had joined it.

He walked, down past the limits of the old Barbary Coast of legendary times, now sanitized into something called an "International Settlement", on into the bustling exotically scented streets of Chinatown which looked much less exotic in the watery sunlight which was struggling to penetrate the dank mistiness of a fine San Francisco morning.

Johnny Kan was already at work in his back office, ploughing into the myriad unepicurean details of restaurant management of which his evening customers would be as unconscious as they would be of the activities of the cleaning crew which was just as busy restoring the dining rooms to the virginal freshness which they would thoroughly debauch before midnight. But he showed no impatience at being interrupted.

"You must have been cheating last night," he said, "or you couldn't look so much better than I feel. Can I do anything for you, or did you only come here to gloat?"

"You can do something for me," said the Saint. "I could do it myself if I had to, but I'm feeling lazy. I'm sure you've got all the connections. Just find out today's schedule for these caramel-cookers that we lost so much beauty sleep dodging last night."

"I must be an all-day sucker," Johnny Kan said, reaching for the phone. "But you had me convinced that it was just a coincidence that you hit San Francisco in the middle of their convention, and you didn't want any part of them."

"I wasn't trying to kid you. The important coincidences have all happened since we said goodnight."

The schedule was forthcoming in a few minutes.

"Ten o'clock, Paramount Theatre: a movie, *New Methods of Merchandising*, followed by a lecture on *Taxation Aspects of the Bottling Industry*. Twelve o'clock, St Francis Hotel, lunch : guest speaker, the President of the San Francisco Chamber of Commerce. Three o'clock, forum : *Soda Fountains and Juvenile Delinquency*. Five o'clock——"

"Whoa," said the Saint. "That's plenty. I only want to know where to look for a guy, and I should be able to find him long before five."

"Would it be very indiscreet to ask which of the caramel-cookers has incurred this unprecedented interest ?"

"No, I don't think so. The name is Otis Q Fennick."

"Oh. Of the Fennick Candy Company ?"

"Why—do you know him ?"

"No. But I know their West Coast representative. A Mr Smith. He eats here sometimes. They have a sales office here, you know."

"I didn't."

"When you want to know anything in a foreign city, you should always consult the natives. Let me look up the address for you. Right now, I should think that's where you'd be most likely to find him. They don't make any soft drinks, so he'd hardly be interested in the tax problems of bottling—if I may presume to offer my amateurish deduction." Kan turned the pages of a city phone book. "Ah, here it is. On Sutter Street—it should be only a block or two from Union Square."

He jotted down the address, and Simon took it gratefully.

"You're right, I'm glad I asked you."

"Doesn't that entitle me to know what this is about?"

"Perhaps, before I leave town, Johnny. But not just yet. There's still too much I haven't figured out myself."

Simon continued his walk, down to Union Square and west on Sutter. The number that Kan had given him was a modern office building, and the directory board in the lobby showed that the Fennick Candy Company was on the second floor. He went up.

From the sequence of doors on the corridor, the West Coast office appeared to take up only two rooms, but they were doubtless sufficient for their purpose. The outer room which he entered contained, besides the standard furniture, a large glass-case display of samples, and a middle-aged woman with an efficient but forbidding air who was typing rapidly at the dictation of some tinny disembodied voice that came through an earphone clamped to her head. Electrically recorded sounds entered her ears and emerged through her fingertips as transformed impulses to be electrically recorded in legible form : she was the only human link in this miracle of technology, and she seemed to bear a deep-rooted grudge against this incurable frailty of hers and to have dedicated herself to suppressing every trace of it that she could.

"Mr Fennick is busy," she said, with a kind of malevolent satisfaction. "Can I help you?"

"I'm afraid not." Simon glanced at the communicating door. "Is he with somebody?"

"Mr Fennick is working on a speech he has to make to the convention tomorrow. He gave the strictest orders that he was not to be disturbed for any reason whatever."

"This is very very important."

"For any reason whatever," the woman repeated smugly.

She was a type that Mrs Fennick would have approved of thoroughly, according to Mr Fennick's thumbnail sketch of his ever-loving spouse. It was as certain as anything humanly could be that she had not sat on anybody's lap since she was knee-high. The paradox that didn't fit at all was that the Liane Fennick whom Simon had met was so utterly unlike his mental picture of a tyrannically jealous wife. But in any puzzle, when all the paradoxes were straightened out, the solution was often absurdly easy.

He inquired patiently : "How long will Mr Fennick be incommunicado?"

"Until five minutes to twelve, when he has to leave for a luncheon."

"Is he always so hard to see?"

"Mr Fennick isn't here very often. And this is a very busy time."

"Is Mr Smith just as busy?"

"Not as a rule. But at present he's covering a meeting for Mr Fennick, since Mr Fennick has to work on his speech. If you'll leave your name and tell me your business, I'll try to arrange an appointment for you."

"Thanks, gorgeous," said the Saint, with beatified earnestness. "I may take you up on that. But later."

He sauntered out.

The next door along the corridor, which displayed only the word PRIVATE under its number, could only be the private entrance to the inner office so zealously guarded by the misanthropic matron with the headset. Even so has many a citadel with intimidating moat and drawbridge had an unguarded postern gate.

Simon leaned an ear against the upper panel. He heard no resonance of rounded phrases in rehearsal, or even the mutter of tentative phrases being fed into a dictating device. Of course, the door might have been exceptionally soundproof, or Mr Fennick might have been a purely cerebral worker. But Simon did not intend to be put off from seeing him, if he was there. It would be easy for the Saint to apologize for having come to the wrong door, which must have been inadvertently left unlocked.

He took from his wallet a wafer-slim implement which he kept there as routinely as another man might have kept a nail file. At this period he seldom needed it as often as twice a year, but he would not have been surprised to have used it twice already that day. And yet on this third possible occasion it finally proved that the Boy Scouts were right and preparedness would always pay off sometime. It slid back the spring lock with less fuss than its own key, and Simon walked in with all the disarming insouciance of the excuse that he had prepared.

He could have saved himself the histrionic warm-up, for there was no audience to be disarmed by it.

The office, except for the traditional appointments of such sancta, was empty.

Simon set the spring lock in the off position, as his story required it, closed the door, and conscientiously forced himself to make another of the definitive checks which seemed to be foisting themselves on him with irksome regularity. Mr Fennick was not in the conveniently coffin-sized coat closet. He was not under or behind the desk. Unless he had been cremated like a moth on the quarter-smoked but cold cigar in the ash tray, or ingested by the mouthpiece of the recording machine which still purred electronically beside the desk, or sucked out through the air conditioner which effectively blockaded the window, he must simply have gone out. Whether his antipathetic amanuensis knew it or not.

The Saint thought that she couldn't know. If she had

known, it would have been just as easy to say he was out, and should have given her the same orgasm of unhelpfulness.

The clock that formed the centrepiece of the onyx inkstand on the desk showed that it still lacked more than twenty minutes of noon.

Simon sat down in one of the guest armchairs, lighted a cigarette, and thought a lot more. For a full two minutes.

Then the outer door opened with the click of a key, and Otis Q Fennick came in.

After the first bounce of his entrance had ploughed to a soggy halt, as if he had bumped into an invisible wall of half-congealed treacle, the lordling of the lollipops looked almost exactly the same as he had when Simon pulled him off the hotel fire escape. That is, he wore the same clothes and the same expression of paralytic befuddlement. The only material difference was that on the former occasion he had been empty-handed, whereas at this moment he was awkwardly lugging under one arm a cardboard carton about the size of a case of Old Curio. This he very nearly dropped as he gaped at the Saint with the reproachful intensity of a gaffed goldfish.

What he said can be loosely reproduced as: "Wha— well—I mean—how——"

"Greetings again, Otis," said the Saint amicably. "I hope you'll forgive me waiting for you like this. Your devoted watchbitch (is that the correct feminine?) insisted that you were busy and wouldn't let me in, but I couldn't tell her why I was sure you wouldn't be too busy to see me. So I toddled around and came in this other door which was fortunately unlatched."

Mr Fennick pushed the door shut, frowning at it.

"I could have sworn I——"

"It must've fooled you," Simon said calmly. "Locks will do that sometimes."

The candy caliph put down his box. It seemed to be moderately heavy, and gave a faint metallic rattle when it tipped.

"Perhaps I didn't check it too carefully," he said. "I only went to the men's room."

"Do you have to take your own pottie?" Simon inquired, gazing pointedly at the carton. "I thought this was quite a modern building."

Mr Fennick also glanced at the box, but seemed to decide against pursuing that subject. He straightened his coat and tie and moved to his desk, pulling himself together with the same air of forced resolution as he might have brought to a difficult business situation.

"Well, now, since you're here," he said, "I hope you didn't think I was ungrateful last night. But the note I left you was intended to be my last word on the subject, Mr Templar."

"That's what I thought," said the Saint. "But what you forgot was that it mightn't necessarily be mine."

"That is what I was afraid of. And that is why I hoped you would be saintly enough to accept my refusal of your services in the spirit in which it was made."

"So you did recognize my name."

"After you'd left me in your room. I had nothing to do but keep on thinking, and it all fitted so well with what I've heard of your reputation. But it also meant that I couldn't afford to be mixed up with you."

"Do you mean because of *your* reputation, or your bank roll?"

"Frankly, because I didn't know how long I could count on your sympathy. If you went on to take an active interest in my problem, I thought, you'd be bound to want to meet my wife eventually, and then she might get you on her side, and I'd be worse off than before. You don't know her, you see, in the same way as I do."

Simon ran lean brown fingers through his dark hair in a vaguely weary gesture.

"As a psychologist, you're a terrific taffy puller," he said. "When I get nosey, it takes more than a polite note to cool me off. And you had me thoroughly intrigued with the plot against your marital honour. So right after breakfast I was baying on the scent you'd let me sniff last night. As a matter of fact, I've just come from the pad of your buxom bedmate, the flashbulb gal."

The other's mouth sagged open to about the same extent as his eyes.

"You saw her?"

"On her way to the morgue. Someone else had been there first, and shot her."

"Are you sure?"

"I didn't see the bullet holes, if that's what you mean. But I saw her carried out, and a neighbour said that's what she died of. However, before that I'd been to the studio of the guy she worked for, to get her address. I had to look it up for myself, in his book. I can vouch for him. Someone made so sure of not missing him that they singed his shirt."

Mr Fennick was still staring rigidly.

"This is shocking!"

"Isn't it? . . . My theory, of course, is that this person went to see Balton for the same reason that I did—to get the gal's address. And also, perhaps, to get the negative of a certain picture. Was the photographer who snapped you in the Don Juan pose a fat fellow with a face like a rather lecherous pig?"

"I was dazed, and blinded by the light, as I told you," Mr Fennick said carefully. "And the man's face was hidden by his camera. But I have a sort of impression that he was stout."

"I'm assuming that Balton was the guy. And since the

gal was on his regular payroll, it would tie in. I also think that with a gun in his ribs he was persuaded to hand over the film, before he got mowed down anyhow."

"Why?"

"Because if he hadn't, there wouldn't't've been any point in killing Norma. She was only worth killing if she'd become the only other person who could swear that there'd ever been such a photo. And with the photo gone, it won't help the police much to be told—as their laboratory boys probably will tell 'em—that the same gun did both jobs. They'll be stuck for a motive, not having the inside dope like us . . . But I saw how you reacted when I told you I'd come from Norma's apartment, before I ever said she'd been shot. And I've noticed that you haven't queried my use of her name and Balton's, although last night you didn't seem to know either one."

Mr Fennick, groping for some occupation for his hands, picked up the spoiled cigar from his ash tray and clamped it between his teeth with a practically unconscious automatism, made a grimace, but re-lighted it anyhow.

"After what I told you last night, Mr Templar, you could make it look very bad for me."

"I could," said the Saint detachedly. "But my problem is that I somehow can't visualize you becoming a murderer just to get out of a phony blackmail jam."

"That's very kind of you."

"So I've been thinking about your wife, and a few things I've learned about her that you didn't tell me. For instance, that she has an old girl friend here, good enough to drop in and stay with. Was this friend's name Uplitz?"

"Oh, no. No. But she does have an old friend here, married to a very successful man in the chemical business."

"Which sounds as if your wife may have lived in San Francisco herself once."

43

"Yes, indeed. This is her home town."

"And she used to be a model."

"Yes."

"So she could have known Vere Balton professionally."

"I suppose it's possible."

"I have another hunch about her. I don't think your married life is exactly blissful. Not that you ever said it was. But I think she'd be happy to get rid of you—if she could only keep enough of the heavy sugar from those Crunchy Wunchies. And you know it, because you're no fool. For the same reason, I think you'd give her her freedom if she'd take a fair settlement. But she's too greedy, so you've been holding out. You could do that if you'd been a good husband and had never given her the usual grounds for divorce."

Mr Fennick's thin mouth was grim and tight around his cigar.

"You're making a lot of personal assumptions, Mr Templar."

"Let me make some more. You weren't worried about her jealous nature, as you led me to believe, but about how much she could take you for if she had the goods on you. And when you recovered from that hit on the head, you figured she'd got 'em. Perhaps you put in a call to your home in New York and found that she'd flown out here yesterday, but without getting in touch with you. That would have cinched it. She could have identified herself as your wife so that even that supercilious young jerk on the desk last night would have given her a spare key to your room, which was all Balton and Norma needed. And you knew you couldn't buy them off, because with that evidence she could match any bid you made. She was all set to take you for everything you've got."

The Candy Company's president had his fingertips pressed to his temples and his thumbs on his cheeks, his hands lightly covering his eyes, in an attitude of intense concentration, and he took no advantage of the moment of silence that Simon offered him.

The Saint got up and walked over to the carton that the other had brought in, giving him time, and lifted the lid inquisitively. What he saw first was a mechanic's cap on top of a crumpled suit of coveralls, which made him suddenly and purposefully delve further. Underneath them he came to the source of the muffled clanking he had heard, a well-worn set of plumber's tools in an open carrier, on top of which was a cheap pair of tinted glasses.

"Well, this fills in a few more blanks," he murmured. "You could have bought the tools at any secondhand store, and the overalls and glasses anywhere, and they make a much better disguise than a false beard. Even if anyone noticed you, the description would never fit Otis Q Fennick, the genius behind Jumbo Juices. Even your colleagues on the convention probably wouldn't recognize you on a fast walk-through. And yet you'd only need a minute in a booth in any public john to change into it or out again. You're just loaded with wasted talent, daddy-o. The only flaw is that you're still stuck with Liane, who could still give the cops that missing motive. One thing leads to another, as the actress tried to warn the bishop when he helped her off with her galoshes."

Mr Fennick sat perfectly still, so that for a second or two Simon seriously wondered whether the accumulated shocks and strains could have been too much for a weak heart.

Then the communicating door burst open, and the surly duenna of the outer office burst in.

For an instant the sheer outraged astonishment of seeing the Saint standing by the desk made her falter in her tracks and almost choked off the words that were piled up to burst from her mouth; but the pressure behind them was too strong.

"I'm sorry, Mr Fennick, but I knew you'd want me to disobey you about this. The hotel called. It's about Mrs Fennick. They were trying to locate you through the convention, and finally they got Mr Smith at the lecture, and he told them you were here. I must warn you, it's something awful——"

"What is it?" Fennick asked.

"She fell out of the window, Mr Fennick. Or she jumped. They seem to think it was suicide!"

"Good God," Fennick said huskily.

Simon stepped forward, between him and his secretary.

"I'll go with him," he said. "You'd better get ready to cope with the reporters. They'll be calling up and flocking around like vultures in no time. But I know you can handle them."

Without actually touching her, he moved her firmly back to the outer office again by the force of increasing proximity alone, and in default of any supporting intervention by her employer she was helpless. The Saint returned her last venomous glare with a winning smile and closed the door on her.

Then he turned back to Fennick and lighted another cigarette.

"I guess I underrated you," he murmured. "You didn't forget about Liane. I suppose she phoned you to gloat over what she thought she'd got and ask if you were ready to talk business again, and you said you'd be right over. The Mercurio is only about three blocks from here, I think, and you could count on that dragon you keep outside to prevent anyone upsetting your alibi. If you had to tap Liane on the head with a wrench to make her easy to push out, the mark wouldn't be noticed after she'd hit the ground, any more than you'd be noticed scooting back down the stairs in your plumber's outfit. You'd reduced all the risks to a minimum, which is the best anyone can do. It was just plain bad luck about me."

The manufacturer moved stiffly around the desk, white-faced but with a certain dignity.

"I'll give myself up," he said. "You needn't come to see that I don't run away."

Simon shook his head reproachfully.

"You're wrong about me again, Otis, old jujube. I think capital punishment is a fine cure for blackmailers. Vere Balton and Norma Uplitz aren't any loss to the community. And that makes your late wife even guiltier than they were. If you can get away with it, good luck to you. The cops won't get any hints from me. I'm only coming along to check out of that crummy hotel and be on my way."

The Fruitful Land

EVEN a champion leads with his chin sometimes, and this was one time when the Saint did it with a flourish and fanfares. He hadn't even been feinted out of position.

"Is there anything I can do for you down in the playgrounds of the Gilded Shmoe?" he asked.

Coming from anyone else, it would have been only a conventional and harmless way of saying thanks for the long weekend of bass fishing that he had enjoyed on the St Johns River between Welaka and Lake George, on his way South to the more sophisticated and in many ways less charming resorts of Florida's Gold Coast. And Jim Harris, the lean and leathery owner of the lodge where Simon Templar always stopped, would have taken it the same way.

"Just don't try to send us everyone you meet," he said good-humouredly. "We've had some good sportsmen and fishermen from down there, but there's some kind that expect more than we're set up to give 'em."

"I know what you mean," Simon said. "A strike on every cast, air-conditioned skiffs, and a gaudy night club to come home to."

They were sitting out on the high bluff overlooking the river, under the magnificent oaks that shaded it in the daytime, after the last dinner of that visit, watching the lights of a tug with a train of barges plodding up the channel and swapping the lazy post-mortems and promises that friends and fishermen swap at such times. At that latitude and inland, the first cold front of fall had spoiled

48

the appetites of the mosquitoes, although it was still only a temporary dispensation that made it enjoyable to stay out after dark.

"On a night like this," Simon murmured idly, "here and now, it's hard to remember what it must have been like for the pioneers who hacked their way through the swamps and jungles of this entomologist's paradise, and made it fit for the non-insect pests to move in."

"I don't think the Spaniards made much out of it," Harris said. "But some of the later carpetbaggers did all right."

"You can say that again," put in his wife, with sudden unwonted vehemence. She turned to the Saint. "Yes, there *is* something you can do—for me, anyway. When you get down around Palm Beach, look up a fellow called Ed Diehl."

"Now, Ernestine——"

"Well, why shouldn't he? The Saint *likes* a good crook to go after, doesn't he? And he might just happen to run short of crooks some wet weekend. And this Diehl is certainly a prize one."

"Now, Ernestine, we can't expect the Saint to take off after any little chiseller who took advantage of——"

"Little chiseller? He's a big chiseller. '*Square*' Diehl, he calls himself, Simon. Hah!"

One of the Saint's redeeming graces was that he knew when he had hooked himself and could accept the consequences gracefully.

"All right," he said placatingly. "I asked for it. What was the deal this merchant got you into?"

"Well, it wasn't long after we started building this place," Jim Harris said. "An aunt of mine back in Texas died and left me four lots she owned somewhere around Lake Worth. We were much too busy getting this place in shape to go down and look at 'em, though I know we could've done it all in a day. We kept telling ourselves we'd have to do it, but somehow we never could find that whole day to spare. A lot of people think that running a camp like this is all play and no work, but you'd be surprised how it ties you down."

"So one day we get a letter from this Diehl," Ernestine said. "He says he's had an inquiry about these lots, and would we be interested in selling. If so, call him collect. He's a regular real-estate broker with a fancy letterhead, so we didn't think there'd be any harm in talking to him."

"He's a real smooth operator," her husband resumed reminiscently. "He soon found out that we'd never been down that way and didn't know much about conditions there, and while he was doing that he'd made himself sound so honest and helpful, I just didn't even doubt him when I asked him what sort of property it was and he said it was in a poor section of town that never had done much good and lots were only fetching about a thousand dollars. I didn't see what he was doing at the time, but I've thought about it since. Right then, when he said he had a customer offering five thousand for the four lots just because they were all together and he was a cranky old guy who didn't want any near neighbours, he made it sound like the last chance we'd ever have to get that kind of price."

"And I can't even say 'I told you so,'" lamented the distaff side of the record. "It sounded just as convincing to me, as you told it, and we thought we were lucky to get a windfall like that just when we could use it."

Simon lighted a cigarette.

"And then you finally made the safari South and saw what you'd sold——"

"No, we still haven't been able to take that day off," Jim said. "But one day we had a couple staying here from Lake Worth, and we got to talking, and right off they said they hoped we hadn't been given a fast shuffle like it seems this Ed Diehl is known for. So I got out the papers, and they knew exactly where these lots were, on a main-road corner right in the middle of a lot of new building developments, and there was a big new supermarket going up now on those very same lots we sold."

"And the old codger who just wanted his privacy?"

"They recognized his name, too. Seems he's a pretty active attorney, not very old, and also a cousin of Mrs Diehl's."

The Saint nodded sympathetically.

"Yes, of course. If a supermarket had appeared as the buyer, you couldn't have helped knowing your property was worth more. They probably sold it to the market out of the same escrow, at a fat profit, without even putting up a dime of their own. And after that first vague letter, I bet you never had anything else from Diehl in writing except the formal 'I enclose herewith' kind of stuff."

"That's right. I realized that when I got mad and started wondering how much I could sue him for. Of all the lies he'd told me, he'd told every one on the telephone. I couldn't prove one thing in a courtroom, except with my word against his."

"He's a sharp operator, all right," Ernestine said. "This couple told us a lot more stories about him. He learned his tricks from his father, who started the business, selling swampland by mail to suckers who never saw it, during the first Florida boom. They had a few square miles that they bought for a dollar an acre, all laid out on paper with streets and business and residential districts and even a city hall, yet, which hasn't been lived in by anything but alligators to this day; but they called it Heavenleigh Hills" —she spelled it out—"and I believe Diehl is still advertising 'retirement farms' there in newspapers far enough away to reach the sort of buyers who'd make a down payment and not come looking for a long while. Anyway, that's the reputation he has locally. But we were the hicks who hadn't heard about it."

"Sure taught me a lesson I won't forget," Jim said ruefully.

"I wish I could be as philosophical as that," said his wife. "I'd just like to see him get his comeuppance, the way the Saint would give it to him."

"I'm the victim of publicity agents I never hired," sighed the Saint. "But for two swell people like you—and in memory of a couple of lunkers that did *not* get away— I'll keep an eye peeled for this square, Diehl."

It was an easy promise to make, of a kind that he had learned to make rather easily in those days when so many people recognized his name or his face and expected miracles of freebooting to be performed instantly. It gave him a respectful inkling of what God must have to cope with if He heard all the prayers. But being only human, in spite of his sobriquet, it must be admitted here and now that Simon sometimes forgot such promises after they had served their first soothing purpose.

The case of Mr Edmund S Diehl happened not to be one of those examples of Saintly fallibility; and that was entirely the fault of Mr Diehl himself. That is, if Mr Diehl had decided at some earlier date to retire with his ill-gotten inheritance added to his own ill-gotten gains and live out his remaining years in luxury in some remote refuge from the tax collectors, the Saint might never have been reminded of him again. Possibly. But Mr Diehl was not a retiring type, and he was entrenched in one of the privileged fields in which tax-heavy Income can be almost effortlessly transmuted into tax-light Capital Gains.

Also, and even more to this point, Mr Diehl had not been raised on poetry. Any landscape, to him, was simply an area of real estate which could be subdivided into smaller areas, with an automatic profit on each reduction, and eventually peddled in convenient building lots at about the same price per foot as it had once brought by the acre. If only God could make a tree, as Mr Diehl had heard it said, Mr Diehl had plenty of bulldozers to knock them down, in his own territory, a lot faster than God could make them. Mr Diehl had effectively demonstrated this over great swaths of fertile soil which his machinery had scraped bare of its natural growth to make room for stark forests of power poles and television antennae brooding over regimented rows of standardized, bleakly functional, and uniformly faceless living-boxes available on a nominal down payment and easy terms. Like almost every other fast-buck Florida developer, Mr Diehl knew exactly what percentage could be saved by scarifying a tract from end to end in steam-roller sweeps instead of wasting time for the blades to manoeuvre in and out among the trees and skin out only the ugly undergrowth. "Landscape", in the only sense he understood it, then became simply a dignified verb for the operation of selling the incoming settlers nursery shrubs and saplings to restock the scorched earth which he had created—a side line which was not to be sneezed at.

Simon Templar had friends of his own to visit in Delray on his way down, and thus it was that his route took him past a pine wood off the main highway which was in course of being swiftly and efficiently razed in the interest of such an improvement as has just been described. He slackened his foot on the speed pedal as he saw the tallest tree in the grove, already canted at a crazy angle, rocking under the ruthless onslaughts of the gaspowered monster butting at its base.

The Florida native pine is a commercially useless tree, disdained as timber, pulpwood, and even fireplace logs. But it will grow slowly, to a fifty-foot height of massive broad-branched thick-leaved evergreen that is one of the few arboreal majesties in a land of shallow contours and generally shallow vegetation. It may take twenty years to do this, so that it is not exactly expendable, except in the most coldly materialistic philosophy.

The Saint thought of himself poetically quite as seldom as Edmund Diehl, but the creaks and groans of the tree and the roars and growls of the steel behemoth worrying it pierced his ears like the sounds of an animate conflict, as his car drifted slowly by; and as the struggle reached its foregone conclusion and the tree toppled and gave up the ghost in a great rending shuddering crash like a stentorian death-rattle, an actual physical hurt seemed to strike deep through his own body. He even trod the car to an abrupt full stop, with a savage insensate impulse to get out and go over and drag the driver out of the bulldozer and smash him down with a fist in the face and drive the bulldozer slowly over him. But he knew just as quickly as he controlled the reflex how stupid and unjust that would have been : the driver was only an innocent and earnest Negro, capably and methodically doing the job that he was paid to do. The man who Simon realized he really wanted was the one who hired the driver and gave him his instructions.

And at that susceptible moment, the Saint looked farther down the road and saw the enormous billboard which proclaimed that this was to be the site of "BLISS HAVEN VILLAGE—*Another Contribution to Florida's Future by* ED (*Square*) DIEHL."

Even if Mr Diehl had been psychically aware of the extra-special attention which he had attracted, it is doubtful if it would have perturbed him. Although he had never outgrown an unquestioning loyalty to his father's corny touch in the naming of projects, he had come a long way since the precarious days of the Heavenleigh Hills promotion. In fact, he had often thought of taking that skeleton out of his closet and burying it, but a certain stubborn cupidity could never quite let him renounce the small but steady revenue that still flaked off its bones. Aside from that, the new boom in Florida land values which began in mid-century had made fabulous profits possible even by legitimate methods, so that Mr Diehl was even accepted as an upstanding member of the community by many citizens with short memories. His dishonesties were mostly neater and mellower than they had formerly been, and always cautiously covered by shrewd legal advice; and such a brazen piece of chicanery as he had perpetrated on Jim Harris was due more than anything to an incurable attitude of mind that would always get the same kind of egotistical lift out of horn-swoggling an unsuspecting victim that a Don Juan type derives from a callous seduction.

Mr Diehl had little else in common with the picture of a Don Juan, being a large gross man with a beefy red face and small piggy eyes as bright as marbles. He wore a very large diamond ring with apparent disregard for the fact that its flashing drew particular attention to his hands, which nearly always featured a set of grimy fingernails; and he had other unpleasant personal habits which would hardly have made him welcome in the best boudoirs. But Mr Diehl, who preferred to base his self-satisfaction on his reception at the bank, was contemplating nothing but rosy futures on a certain morning when one of his underlings sidled into his private office and told him that there was a potential client outside whom he might want to see.

"The Count of Cristamonte, yet. And he's looking for a big deal."

Mr Diehl had a plentiful staff of salesman and secretaries to handle routine and minor transactions, but he had it understood that the most important properties were handled by himself personally. In this way he could entitle himself to pocket more of the commission, and also give himself more to brag about at the Golf Club bar.

"Then send him in, boy, send him in."

The client had about him a quiet aroma of potential moola that Mr Diehl recognized at once. He carried himself with the graceful and unhurried confidence of one who is accustomed to deference, and his blue eyes had the easy nonchalance that nothing buttresses quite so solidly as the spare figures in a bank account; and if the trim pointed beard that outlined his lean jaw gave him a somewhat rakish and piratical appearance, that impression was softened by the mild and engaging way he spoke. It was a characterization to which the Saint had lately become quite attached, and it had yet to have its first failure.

"What kind of price range were you thinking in?" Mr Diehl asked bluntly, as soon as he could bluntly ask it.

"I don't think there are any ordinary limits," Simon said calmly. "I represent a syndicate of European investors who happen to have very large dollar credits to dispose of and would like to keep their capital working in this prosperous country."

"What type of property are they interested in? Income, or development?"

"For a start, we were thinking of a country club that might be the most exclusive in America—strictly for what I think you call 'rich millionaires'. It would have to be on the Ocean, for the beach, and also on the waterway, for a private yacht harbour; and besides the usual bungalows and restaurant it would naturally need room for its own tennis courts, golf course, polo field, bridle trails, private airport, and so on. We could easily use two or three thousand acres. And if the property was right, we should not haggle over a million dollars one way or the other."

Mr Diehl cleared his throat and aimed a sloppy shot at the brass cuspidor beside his desk, to prove that it was not just an antique ornament and that making light of a million dollars did not necessarily awe him.

"A hunk of property like that is going to take a bit of finding, these days, with all the subdividing that's been going on——"

"I'm well aware of that," said the Saint. "And so I shall naturally be asking all the important brokers what they have to offer. You just happen to be the first one on my list. Eventually I shall have to deal with the one who has the most suitable parcel to show me. I hope there's no misunderstanding about that."

"Now let's think that through, Count," said Mr Diehl, scratching himself vigorously, which he was given to doing when he was excited. "I don't want to talk out of turn, but you probably haven't any idea how many highbinders there are in this business. You're lucky you came to me first. Everyone knows what they call *me* around here: 'Square' Diehl—it's right out there on the front of the building. But what they call some of the others I wouldn't want to quote to you."

"Indeed?"

"Yes, sir. And if there's any kind of buyer they'll gang up on worse than a Yankee, it's a foreigner, if you'll excuse the word. Maybe you were thinking that if you shop around, you'd have 'em all competing to offer you the best property at the best price. Well, you'd be wrong. They've worked out a better system than cutting each other's throats. They've got an unofficial combine, and what they'd do is pass the word along, and every one would jack up the price of everything to you, and whoever you bought through they'd split the difference. In that way, everybody gets a commission—and you'd be paying all ten or fifteen of 'em instead of one."

"But that's almost crooked!" exclaimed the Saint, in shocked accents.

"You can say that again. But we can beat 'em—if you'd let me have this exclusive for a while."

"How?"

Mr Diehl spat again, almost missing the brass bowl in his haste.

"Like this. Besides checking everything on our books that looks promising, I'll have my salesmen contact all the other real estate offices, but very casually, without mentioning any names, see? That way, we'll get an honest price on everything that might suit you that anyone has got listed. And then when it comes to making an offer, I'll get a friend of mine who lives here to put in the bid, and they'll know they can't fool him with any fancy prices, but of course he'll make an agreement in advance to sell the property to your syndicate at just a reasonable mark-up for his trouble."

"That sounds like an interesting idea. But what have I done to deserve so much help from you?"

"Just blame it on the way I was brought up, Count. My father, who founded this business, used to tell me, God rest him, 'I never want anyone who walks in these doors to walk out saying he didn't get a square deal.' If I find you what you want and make the sale, I'll be perfectly satisfied."

The Saint had no doubts whatsoever on that score, but did not judge the moment opportune to press Mr Diehl for details as to how this satisfaction would be achieved. He simply allowed himself to look deeply impressed by a revelation of corrupt practices which might well have made the collective hair of the Florida Real Estate Board stand on end if its members had heard it. Mr Diehl did not even give that a thought, since there were no witnesses, and in any case there were a score of ways to explain how an ignorant foreigner might have misunderstood him.

"I'm very glad to have met you, Mr Diehl," Simon said

with unaffected sincerity. "And I think I shall give your suggestion a try. Instead of contacting other agents this weekend, as I had planned, I shall let you do the work—while I go fishing, which to be truthful I much prefer."

"You won't regret it, I promise you. I'll put my whole staff to work on it. While you go fishing. Have you arranged for a boat? I can get you the very best sailfish captain in these waters——"

"Pardon, but I was not thinking of the ocean fishing, though I know how wonderful it is here. But I have done so much of it—from Panama to Peru to New Zealand, you understand. Here in the southeast United States I like to fish one thing only, for which even in your country this is the headquarters, and which the rest of the world does not even know—the big-mouth bass."

"The greatest fishing in the world," Mr Diehl concurred automatically.

"I have studied it very closely, and I think on this visit I must catch a record. At any rate I shall enjoy proving my theory. Perhaps you yourself are a bass fisherman, Mr Diehl?"

"There's nothing in the world I like better, except you-know-what."

Ed ('Square') Diehl would have given the same answer, with the same leer and wink, to any customer with the same profit potential, on any subject from baseball to Balinese dancing in which the customer expressed an interest.

"I've had a theory for a long time," Simon pursued, with a somewhat Countly portentousness, "that the reason why it begins to be said that your Florida waters are fished out—is that they are. The new roads that go everywhere, the new cars that everyone has, the new boats and outboards that everyone can afford on instalments—all this had placed an unbelievable pressure on the fish, who do not have similar devices on their side. Therefore there are no important bass left to catch where anyone can go. But for some privileged sportsmen there will always be some wilderness that is still fruitful in the old way, which modern science can make accessible. Here in Florida, in spite of your fantastic coastal developments, you are still only on the perimeter of a sportsman's paradise to which the new key is—the helicopter!"

"You got something there, Count."

"I am betting I have, Mr Square. You take off even today, in your helicopter, in spite of all the highways and turnpikes, and in less than half an hour you can be fishing where the fish have never seen anyone but a Seminole. I would like to show you this. I happen to have a small private helicopter which I bought to inspect properties; and if you like, this weekend, since I shall not be consulting other sharkers—I beg your pardon, *brokers*—you should come with me as a good fisherman and let me prove this."

Mr Diehl thought quickly, which he could always do when the chips were down, and did not have to be any unusual genius to realize that a Count of Cristamonte anywhere in the wilds with him would certainly be worth more than the same perambulating exchequer exposed to the sales pitch of the next grifter who might glom on to him.

"That's a great idea," Mr Diehl said, wriggling inside his sodden shirt. "My staff will spend the weekend getting a line on every big tract in this and the next two counties, while you and me get a line on them bass."

It was not to be expected that Mr Diehl would fail to let it leak out as widely as possible that he was going fishing in the private plane of no less an international personage than the Count of Cristamonte, and as a matter of fact the Saint was counting on it as a minor but useful contribution to his plan. Nor was he disappointed or disconcerted when Mr Diehl's belated qualms at the imminence of entrusting his life to the skill of an unknown pilot, and a foreigner at that, caused the realtor to make himself unusually conspicuous at the County airfield by the noisy irreverence and raucous humour with which he tried to cover up his misgivings and convince the mechanics who were servicing the whirlybird that such expeditions were as commonplace to him as a trip to the bathroom. Simon Templar never omitted such factors from his calculations, and Mr Diehl lived up to everything that he expected.

After a vertical take-off they first headed roughly south, and then swung west somewhere over the outskirts of Delray. In only a few minutes the dense development of the coastal strip had faded into a hazy horizon and they were over a weird incredibly flat-looking wilderness of scrubby green dappled with myriad patches of water and sometimes scored with the thin straight slash of a drainage canal. This was the perspective that is always a little startling, when the blank spaces that take up most of the map of the lower Florida peninsula become a visible wilderness, and it can actually be seen how comparatively insignificant a rim of civilization has even yet been established on the raw land that is still straining to hold itself a few precarious feet out of the sea.

Ed Diehl had seen this vista before, or other areas indistinguishable from it, from the windows of large commercial airliners approaching the ports of West Palm Beach or Miami, without thinking even that much about it, for he was not an imaginative man except when describing some property or proposition that he was trying to sell; but before long he began to feel something radically unfamiliar about the view he was getting of it today, and in another little while it dawned on him that the important difference was one of altitude. The big passenger planes roared over at speeds that dwarfed the empty distances, and came slanting down into the serried suburbs from heights that hardly let one landmark out of sight before another could be identified. Whereas the helicopter, after crossing the split ribbon of the new turnpike at no more than three hundred feet, had gradually let down until it was cruising at what might have been little more than treetop height, if there had been any trees important enough to judge by. Mr Diehl was aware that they made a number of changes of direction, as the copter obeyed the impulses of its pilot with some of the irresponsibility of a mechanical hummingbird; but the noise of the rotors made conversation difficult, and Mr Diehl did not want to seem fussy or uneasy, so he confined himself to grinning occasionally and trying to look as if he were enjoying every minute.

When the engine note finally changed a little, and the helicopter tilted to a standstill and settled slowly to the ground like a rather unsteady elevator, Mr Diehl would not even have bet on which county he was in. His last orientation point had been some distant watery horizon that could equally well have been the Atlantic Ocean or the forty-mile diameter of Lake Okeechobee: he had not been watching the compass, and in any case he was vague about the turns they had made since then. But the Count seemed to know what he was doing, and when the overhead blades had shuddered to silence Mr Diehl turned to him in a passable impersonation of a man who had gone along on a dozen or two similar expeditions.

"You sure know how to drive this egg-beater, Count," he said.

"Luckily for us," said the Saint, unbuckling his safety belt and climbing out. "If anything happened to me, it wouldn't be any more use to you than a kid's tricycle for getting out of here, would it?"

"You can say that again," grinned Mr Diehl.

"And what chance do you think you'd have of making it on foot?"

Mr Diehl gazed around. They were near the edge of one of the small lakes or large ponds that were visible everywhere from the air. The ground where they had landed and immediately around where they stood felt firm underfoot, but not far away water glistened between blades of sedge that would have looked like dry land from above. And everywhere else was nothing but the endless rippling expanse of wild grass varied sometimes by a fringe of reeds or a clump of palmettos, and broken only by an occasional scrawny tree or tuft of cabbage palm or the bare ghostly trunk of a dead cypress. Mr Diehl tried not to let it impress him.

"I'm glad I won't have to try."

"Then," said the Saint calmly, "I guess you won't care how much I charge for flying you out."

Mr Diehl laughed heartily—not because he saw the joke, but because he thought he was supposed to.

"I should say not. What's your price?"

"At this moment, only forty thousand dollars."

Mr Diehl laughed again, a little more vaguely.

"That's mighty generous of you."

"I'm glad you think so," said the Saint, and thereupon took his spinning rod out of the cabin and cautiously explored a route to the edge of the open water and began to fish.

Mr Diehl watched him somewhat puzzledly for a few minutes, and then decided that such incomprehensible foreign pleasantries were hardly worth racking his brain over. He fetched his own rod and tackle box and found a place a little farther along to try some casting himself.

It is possible that the bass in that remote slough were every whit as innocent and unspoiled as the Count of Cristamonte had theorized, but after a time it began to seem that even if they had never learned to suspect a hook they had grown up with much the same dumb instincts and habits as other bass, a species which does most of its feeding at dusk and dawn and is inclined to spend the heat of the day digesting or snoozing or holed up in finny meditation. At any rate, a wide variety of lures and retrieves failed to get either of them a strike, and Mr Diehl himself could recognize that the only signs of activity that broke the glassy water were made by gar. But as the sun rose higher and hotter and the bass presumably sank deeper into their cool weedy retreats, Mr Diehl grew thirstier, and began to think longingly of the supply of beer which he had seen loaded onto the helicopter in a portable icebox.

As if in telepathic unanimity, he saw the Count heading back at last to the ship, and hastened to join him.

"That," he said, smacking his lips as he watched the puncturing of a can dripping with cool moisture, "is going to taste awful good."

"It certainly is," Simon agreed, and proceeded to prove it to himself.

Mr Diehl was very faintly aware of something less than the elaborate olde-worlde courtesy he had read about somewhere, but he cheerfully reached in to grab and open his own can, and was duly startled to find his movement barred by a steel-cored arm.

"Just a minute, chum," said the Saint. "Beer is selling here for a thousand dollars a shot."

Mr Diehl's grin this time was a trifle laboured.

"Okay," he said. "I'll owe it to you."

"I'm sorry, but I can't give credit. After all, my price is

64

strictly based on how much the customer might be willing to pay at the moment."

"You should of told me before we left, and I'd of brought some cash with me."

"Oh, I'm not as difficult as that. Your cheque is good enough."

"Too bad I didn't bring my cheque-book either."

"I was afraid you mightn't, so I brought one for you. This is one of your banks, isn't it?"

Mr Diehl stared stupidly at the printed pad that was conjured almost from nowhere to be flourished under his nose. In the circumstances, he was prepared to extend himself almost infinitely to be a good joe and go along with a gag, but this was rapidly getting beyond him.

"Yes, it is," he said strenuously. "But frankly, Count, I must apologize if I missed the joke somewhere——"

"Suppose you start getting back on the beam by dropping that 'Count' business, Ed," Simon suggested kindly, and it was only then that he shed the last vestiges of an accent which had been getting progressively thinner with every sentence. "I'm going to give you a big moment for your memoirs. I am the Saint, and I'm giving you the priceless favour of my personal attention in this project of collecting a small assessment which I've decided that you should pay on your ill-gotten gains."

"You sound crazier every minute," Mr Diehl mumbled, though in a still crazier way this was beginning to sound like the most real nightmare he had ever experienced. "So you're the Saint. Some kind of fancy crook. All right, you kidnapped me——"

"I don't remember it that way," Simon corrected him genially. "There was no violence or intimidation. In fact, you told everyone who'd listen to you at the airport how much you were going to enjoy this trip with me."

"But if you keep me here——"

"I never said I wanted to keep you here. I merely told you how much I'd charge to fly you out. That's my privilege, as a free agent in a free country."

Mr Diehl glared at him through a kind of fog. There was a purely mental haze as well as the emotional murk in it, steaming off a much larger mass of incredibilia than his limited mentality could assimilate at one gulp. *a*) The Saint was only a mythological character anyhow; and *b*) even if he wasn't, this couldn't be happening to him, Ed Diehl; and *c*) even if it was happening, there must be some flaw in the structure of such an outrageous swindle. But for the moment the lean corsair's face and figure that confronted him were fantastically convincing.

"You won't get a nickel out of me," he said, and tried to overcome an infuriating feeling of futility. "You and your Count of Cristamonte story——"

"I didn't try to get a nickel out of you with that story," said the Saint virtuously, "because that would have been fraudulent. But there's nothing illegal about using a phony name just for fun." He drank again from the can, deeply and with relish, and then made another raid on the icechest for a square plastic box, from which he extracted a thick and nourishing sandwich. "Pardon me if I have lunch," he said. "There are plenty more of these, by the way, and to you they are only two thousand dollars each."

Mr Diehl could not have explained why this was the precise twitch that snapped the rein of his congenitally crude and choleric temper, but it was probably far more a general sense of frustration than any specific affront that made him crowd forward again with his fists bunched and his face purpling.

"I'm not taking any of this crap," he growled. "You give me a sandwich *and* a can of beer, or I'll help myself!"

"You're standing in the shade of my helicopter," Simon pointed out forbearingly. "For using this very expensive piece of equipment as a parasol I shall have to make a charge of one hundred dollars a minute. If you think that's too high and you want to get out of the sun, go and sit under a tree."

"*What* tree?" roared Mr Diehl.

"Oh, there don't seem to be any right around here, now you mention it. But you don't care much about trees anyway, do you? At least, when they're in the way of a fast cheap cleanup job on a subdivision, you're the type of clot-headed dollar-clutching slob who——"

That was the exact moment when Mr Diehl threw his Sunday punch, and perhaps it was just bad luck that this was only Saturday.

The Saint did not let go either the can of beer which he held in one hand or the sandwich in the other, but he leaned a little to one side and brought up an elbow with the power and accuracy of a short uppercut; and Mr Diehl suddenly found himself lying on his back with a numb sensation in his jowls, a taste of blood in his mouth, and an astronomically unrecorded nova erupting in the red haze that had temporarily clouded his vision.

With even more care not to spill a drop or lose a crumb, Simon used one foot to roll the realtor out into a rather muddy expanse of sunlight.

"Just for that gratuitous display of bad temper," he said, "the fee for flying you out has now gone up to fifty grand."

Mr Diehl sat on a damp log in the sun, making it damper with his own sweat, after the Saint had finished eating and drinking and had stretched himself out for a siesta under the shadow of the helicopter. Glowering at him from a safe distance, Mr Diehl had inevitably toyed with the idea of a murderous sneak attack; but when he was recovered enough to make the first tentative move in that direction, he was instantly greeted by the opening of a cool catlike eye which without any other explanation at all convinced him that such a manoeuvre would not have the automatic success it might have conveniently enjoyed in a story.

In any case, even if he could have overpowered the Saint, he didn't know how he could have forced him to fly the helicopter. A man might be beaten or even tortured into promising to fly; but once in the air, the passenger was at the mercy of the pilot. And if the preliminary struggle actually incapacitated or even killed the Saint, Mr Diehl would still be stuck there until a rescue party found him, and it could be a long time before any such search was organized. He recalled now, with awful clarity, how the Saint had told the airport crew that they expected to spend at least three days in the Everglades and might even go on to explore some of the inaccessible islands of the Bay of Florida before turning back—to all of which misdirection Mr Diehl had contributed his loud support.

Far out beyond the last stems of maiden cane, something dark and gnarled came slowly awash in the glazed surface of the water. Mr Diehl identified it after a while as the front end of an alligator, which stared at him with inscrutable agate eyes. Mr Diehl stared back, somewhat less enigmatically, and remembered to wish that he had brought a gun.

There had to be some weak point in the set-up, if he could only find it.

The Saint came languidly back to life, yawned and stretched, smoked a cigarette, bathed his face with a cloth ostentatiously dipped in ice-water from the cooler, hauled out a sheaf of magazines, and sat down again in the shade to read.

"You're crazy," Mr Diehl shouted.

"It just isn't the time of day to catch bass," argued the Saint reasonably. "As a native of these parts, you ought to know that. So I'm improving my mind instead of tiring out my arm. Would you care to join me? I'm renting magazines at only a hundred dollars a minute for the reading kind, or two hundred for the ones with girlie photos."

Mr Diehl clenched his teeth to the point of almost cracking some expensive bridgework, but managed to suppress an answer that would have been impractical and unprofitable.

He was sharply susceptible to hunger, like any man accustomed to self-indulgence and a high-calorie diet, but he also had a cushion of accumulated blubber that could absorb temporary deprivations without acute distress. Mr Diehl felt miserably empty in the stomach, but in no danger of fainting from it. The thirst was much harder to bear. His propensity for profuse sweating was always a strain on his fluid resources, and the thought of cold cans of beer nestling in arctic beds of ice cubes or dripping clean refreshing wetness as they were lifted out was a re-fined anguish that became more acute with the passing of each unslaked minute. It got so bad that even while his pores were acting like faucets he could hardly find enough internal moisture for a good spit.

When the sun began to cooperate by dousing itself pre-maturely behind a high bank of clouds in the west, the Saint finished another can of beer and began fishing again. After a while he tied on to a fish that erupted from the water like a stung dervish as it felt the hook, and fought through several more minutes of explosive leaps and straining runs before the light tackle could subdue it. Mr Diehl watched morosely while the Saint beached it and unhooked it and held it up with a skilful thumb under its jaw.

"Would you like it for supper, Ed? Only two thousand dollars!"

"You go to hell," Mr Diehl said hoarsely.

"Just as you like, Ed," said the Saint agreeably.

He put the bass gently back in the water and released it. Then he slapped at himself a couple of times, and picked his way back to the shallow mound where the helicopter stood.

The word "picked" is not just an idle choice. At one point he froze abruptly on one foot, and remained thus grotesquely poised for several seconds, while a water moccasin slowly unwound its thick black coils from around the tuft of grass that he had been about to step on and slithered off into the muck. Mr Diehl saw it, and wondered if the Saint was also equipped with antivenin, and how much a shot would cost anyone else.

"The mosquitoes are starting to get hungry," Simon observed imperturbably, slapping himself again.

Mr Diehl had already noticed that. He squirmed and fanned himself savagely while the Saint leaned into the cabin and brought out a bottle of insect repellent.

"I don't want to rush you, Ed," Simon remarked, rubbing himself liberally with the lotion, "but we don't seem to be getting anywhere, and pretty soon I'm going to weaken for the idea of a nice cold shower, some clean clothes, a tall tinkling Pimm's Cup in an air-conditioned bar, a prime steak dinner, and a comfortable bed. If you haven't given in before I do, I guess I'll just have to leave you here and hope I can find you again tomorrow." He replaced the cap on the bottle. "Would you like some of this gunk? You can have it for only five grand, and before morning you'll think it was cheap at the price."

Mr Diehl's small eyes grew bigger with horror. The last straw that breaks the camel's back is a time-worn cliché, but something like it happened to whatever stubbornness

70

he had left. The unappetizing brown swamp water was certainly drinkable if a man got thirsty enough, and nobody died of simple starvation in a few days. But the prospect of a night of utter loneliness in the teeming dark, surrounded by snakes and alligators, with myriads of small swift invisible stinging and biting things to add real torment to imagination, was already a living nightmare before which the edges of his pampered brain curled in clammy panic.

"You wouldn't do that," he croaked. "A man could be killed or go nuts in one night, left here like that."

"A Seminole wouldn't mind it a bit," contradicted the Saint. "But if it doesn't appeal to you, you don't have to stay."

Mr Diehl knew it. And in that moment of truth, he also saw the elementary answer that had eluded him for so many wretched hours, and could scarcely believe that he had been so stupid as to miss it in the first five minutes.

"You're right, I don't," he said. "Give me that repellent. And the cheque-book. And while I'm writing the cheque, get me a can of beer."

"You could probably use a sandwich, too, to hold you till you get home," said the Saint. "Let's call it fifty-five thousand for the whole works, since you're paying it all at once."

Mr Diehl scribbled the cheque, and would not have cared much what the exact figures were. But the Saint examined it carefully before he folded it and put it away in his wallet.

"You may wonder why I should take all this trouble, when it might have been easier just to forge your signature," he said. "But for some years now I've been trying to go straight, as the phrase has it, and I don't want to be accused of doing anything criminal to get your money."

Mr Diehl drained the can of beer in three long gulps,

and scratched himself almost joyously. He was beginning to think that this highly publicized Saint character might literally have a weak place in his head, which it had taken a smart and nerveless man like Ed Diehl to discover.

"I just hope you get a sympathetic jury when you have to justify your prices," he felt bold enough to say.

"Everyone is entitled to his day in court," said the Saint equably. "And to save a lot of time-wasting argument there, I think we ought to mark this historic spot."

He turned the cheque book over and wrote quickly on the back of the last cheque:

> *This is the place that I paid $55,000 to be flown out of.*

"Sign it," he said, "and I'll witness it."

This was done; and the note was sealed inside the plastic sandwich box, which was buried under the cypress log on which Mr Diehl had spent a good part of his unhappiest day. But he was far from unhappy as the whirling blades overhead brought the reassuring geometric patterns of highway and building in sight again, and in an absurdly few minutes the runways of the Lantana airfield were rising towards them out of the dusk.

He opened the door on his side and jumped out the moment the helicopter touched down, and was slightly ecstatically amazed that the Saint made no attempt to grab him. He did not fall on his knees and kiss the firm concrete under him, not being that kind of emotional jerk; but nothing could have stopped him taking a stand directly he had backed off beyond probable recapture or reprisal, and shouting his ultimate triumph and defiance.

"You sonofabitch!" he bawled. "Don't waste time trying to cash that cheque after the cops get through working you over, because I'll be at the bank when it opens on Monday to stop payment!"

Simon cut the engine and leaned out so as not to have to compete in vulgar volume.

"Okay, Ed," he said gently. "You play it the way you see it. But long before that I'll have flown in a load of witnesses to pick up our X-marks-the-spot, and they'll all be qualified surveyors who can testify that we buried it right where your plat calls for the City Hall of a dream town called Heavenleigh Hills. It should make fabulous publicity for everything else you're contributing to the Future of Florida. Anyhow, you've got all tomorrow to think it over."

Mr Diehl's petulant baby face, grubby and scorched and sweat-streaked, puckered slowly but exactly like the face of a spoiled child about to burst into tears. It was an expression that the Saint had seen before. He hoped he would see it many times again.

The Percentage Player

THERE is a story, which may be apocryphal, about a certain bookmaker (of the horsey, not the literary, variety) who was making a long trip by car when towards nightfall he happened upon a hostelry which displayed an ordinary sign bearing a most unusual name, *The Even Steven*.

To a man in his business, this quaint appellation was of course doubly intriguing ; and since it was in the middle of a particularly bleak and desolate stretch of country, and he had no idea how much farther he might have to drive to find a meal and a bed, he quickly decided to stop there for the night and satisfy his curiosity at the same time. The proprietor soon explained the peculiar designation of the place.

"It's very simple, really. You see, my name actually is Steven Even. So I just decided to turn it around and call this *The Even Steven*. I thought it might get a few folks puzzled enough to stop and ask questions, and sometimes it does. Like yourself."

"That's a pretty smart way to use the luck of a name," said the bookie appreciatively. "I bet it brings you a lot of business."

Mr Even, a dour and dejected type of individual, seemed glad to have someone to talk to.

"It hasn't brought me so much luck," he said. "The folks who stop don't stay long. There's not much gaiety around here, as you could see. In fact, there's not another soul lives closer than thirty miles away, whichever way you go. Makes it pretty lonely for me, a widower. And worse still for my daughters. Three of the loveliest girls you ever set eyes on, should have their pick of boy friends. But the nearest lads would have to drive thirty miles to pick 'em up, thirty more to take 'em to a movie, thirty miles to bring 'em home, and thirty back themselves. That's more 'n they got time to do even for beauties like these. The girls are getting so frustrated they're about ready to do anything for a man."

The bookie made sympathetic noises, and listened to more in the same vein until hunger obliged him to change the subject to that of food. An excellent home-cooked dinner was served to him by a gorgeous blonde who introduced herself as Blanche Even; and when he was surfeited she still kept pressing him to ask for anything else he wanted.

"A toothpick, perhaps?" he suggested.

She brought it, and said : "Would you like me to sit and talk to you for a while?"

"Thank you," he said politely, "but I've had a long day and I feel like closing the book."

He went to his room, and had just started to undress when there was a knock at the door and an absolutely breath-taking brunette came in.

"I'm Carmen Even," she said. "I just wanted to see if you'd got everything you want."

"I think so, thank you," he said pleasantly. "I do a lot of travelling, so I pack very systematically."

When he had finally convinced her and got rid of her, he climbed in between the sheets and was preparing to read himself to sleep over the *Racing Form* when the door opened again to admit an utterly stupefying redhead in a négligée to end all négligées.

"I'm Ginger Even," she announced. "I wanted to be sure your bed was comfortable."

"It is," he assured her.

"I hope you're not just being tactful," she insisted. "May I try it myself?"

"If you must," said the bookie primly. "I will get out while you do it."

When she had gone, he settled down with a sigh of relief and was about to put out the light at last when the door burst open once more and the proprietor himself stomped in, glowing with indignation.

"What's the matter with you?" he roared. "I got to listen all night to my daughters moaning an' wailing, the most lusciousest gals in this county, because they all try to show you hospitality an' you won't give one of 'em a tumble. Ain't us Evens good enough for you?"

"I'm sorry," said the transient. "But I told you when I registered, I'm a professional bookmaker. I only lay Odds."

Mr Theocritus Way, this chronicler must now hasten to establish, was not the bookie immortalized in the foregoing anecdote. He was, however, a man who had concentrated on the subject of Odds with an almost comparably classic single-mindedness.

Indeed, one of his oldest but perennially profitable discoveries in the field was directly tied to the same numerical quibble between Odds and Evens. At any bar where he might be chumming for potential suckers, when the inevitable dispute eventually arose as to who should buy another drink, he would promptly suggest that they match for it. The mark could hardly refuse this, and would take from his pocket the conventional single coin. Mr Way would then say, with a skilfully intangible sneer : "The hell with that penny-matching stuff. That's how some guys got rich making double-headed coins. Let's play Monte Carlo Match."

He always had some high-sounding name, suggestive of authenticity and tradition, for the games that he invented.

"What's that?" the innocent would ask.

Mr Way would haul out a handful of small change, which he jingled noisily in his closed fist to leave no doubt that it was a fair quantity.

"I got a mess of chickenfeed here," he would explain, with laboured patience for such ignorance. "You grab a stack from your own pocket. We slap it all on the bar— two stacks. Suppose your stack turns out to be an odd number, and the total of our two stacks is also an odd number, you win. Suppose you got an odd number, and the total of us two is even, you lose. Or vice versa. That's one bet you can't fix, because neither of us knows how many coins the other's going to have."

The mark might win or lose the first time, on this fair fifty-fifty basis. Mr Way rather liked him to win, because that made it somewhat easier to insist on another match for money instead of drinks. And one game easily led to another, and another, for increasing stakes. If the dupe insisted on them taking turns as matcher, Mr Way would take his honest fifty-fifty chance. But after the first time, the victim never had a chance to match the total of their combined hands in oddness or evenness.

Whenever the other was trying to "match," Mr Way simply took care to have some odd number of coins in his own stack. Therefore if the mug also had an odd number, the joint total had to be even. Stated this way, any intelligent reader will see that the stupe would have had the same fifty-fifty chance of finding somebody with a right foot growing naturally on his left leg. But it was a gimmick which had paid Mr Way more cash dividends than Albert Einstein ever earned from the Theory of Relativity.

The fond parent who had him baptized Theocritus was only another of the human race's uncounted casualties to misguided optimism. Even in his tenderest years, his contemporaries declined to accord him even the semi-dignified contraction of "Theo." They abbreviated him swiftly and spontaneously to "Tick." The record does not show whether this was initially due to his instinct for stretching credit to the snapping point whenever he was supposed to do the paying, to his physically insignificant stature, or to his extraordinary irritating personality; or to a combination of all three. But the monicker clung to him like flypaper into the middle-aged maturity where his path crossed the Saint's, which is the only encounter this short story is seriously concerned with.

However, in contradiction of some recent propaganda which purports to attribute all adult crime to the cancerous frustration of the growing boy, it must be instantly said that "Tick" Way consistently collected above-average grades, and revealed an especial talent for mathematics. But instead of being thus inspired to think of a career in science or engineering, his temperament had been impressed only by the magnificent possibilities of pigeon-plucking that were opened up by the magical craft of figures.

In his middle forties he was still a runt, barely topping five feet in his built-up shoes, but broad and thick-set and now somewhat paunchy, a strutting little rooster of a man with all the aggressiveness with which the small ones are prone to over-compensate for their unimpressive size, and a toughly amorphous face which looked as if he had antagonized more than one person whose resentment was too convulsive to be conveyed without physical amplification. But if he was doomed by his chromosomes to be forever unformidable in a fight, he had a grasp of the immutable laws of probability that might have frightened an insecurely wired electronic brain.

For "Tick" Way, the comparatively obvious percentages of dice were teen-age stuff. He had nothing but contempt for the half-sharp crapshooters who knew that the true odds were three to one against a natural on the first roll, two to one against making a point of ten, and thirty-five to one against making it the hard way—only because they had read the figures in a book. He could work out all those simple chances in his own head and even knew how to project them into the more elaborate calculation which ends up showing that the shooter has only a 49·3% chance of passing when he takes the dice.

The higher complexities of poker were not much harder for him. He did not have to memorize the odds of twenty-three to one against drawing two cards to make a flush, or ninety-seven to one against drawing three cards that would turn a pair into a full house. He could even prove on paper the paradoxical theorem that when holding two pairs against an opponent who you are sure has threes, you have a better chance of taking the pot if you discard your smaller pair and buy three new cards than if you timidly trade your maverick for just one that you hope will fill the hand.

Mr Way had long since relegated such overworked games to the category of minor pastimes or last resorts. For one thing, he had also learned a few things about the mechanical methods of loading, shaving, switching, marking, and otherwise hocusing cards and dice, to say nothing of the sleights of hand (for which he himself had no natural aptitude whatever) in their manipulation, which could nullify the most comprehensive theoretical calculations. For another, he had found that a discouraging percentage of even the most verdant greenhorns had been forewarned through the modern media of Sunday newspaper supplements, paperback fiction, B pictures and television, of the hazards of playing games with strangers. And thirdly, the relatively fractional edge that a brain with a built-in slide rule might give him in conventional gambling was too small and laborious in the payola to satisfy his driving ambitions. He would prefer to cash in any day on some proposition in which his advantage could be measured not in fractions but in fat round numbers.

Simon Templar first saw him in action at the bar of the Interplanetary Hotel in Miami Beach. Every season during this era of seemingly endless expansion saw the opening of some gleaming new caravanserai which aspired to be the "hotel of the year"—bigger, grander, gaudier, more modern, more luxurious, and more expensive than all the jampacked hundreds of other palaces to which it added its opulence—which for a few dizzy months would skim the cream of the traffic before it yielded to the hotel of next year which was even then in the girder stage on the adjoining lot. The period of this story is fatally pinpointed by the mere mention of the Interplanetary Hotel, which obviously staked its début on the fact that solemn citizens who once automatically dismissed science fiction as a form of juvenile escapism were currently pontificating about rockets to the moon and pondering the legal tricks that might have to be invoked to grab off the largest hunk of the lunar market. The entrepreneurs of this palatial pub had already nailed their seats on the bandwagon by having the lobby laid out on the lines of some futuristic concept of a space port, decorating the main dining room with symbols aimed at striking a happy compromise between astronomy and astrology, branding their plushier accommodations with such labels as "The Martian Suite" or "The Venusian Suite," and barely stopping short of putting Plexiglas bubble helmets on the bellboys. And for that season, at least, they were assured of entertaining the loudest, lushest, most ostentatious fugitives from the northern snows who were likely to get washed up on that excessively upholstered strand. The ideal subjects, in fact, for Mr Way's studiously honed technique.

This was one of those rare but reliable drizzling grey afternoons which the Chamber of Commerce sweeps furiously under the rug, but which stubbornly re-manufacture themselves a few times every winter—the kind of day which makes even the stiffest isolationists tend to unbend in the common misery of being done out of most of the highly advertised amenities while paying the same $50 daily rent on a minimum room. Mr Way hit the bar (or the Spaceship Room, as the brochures called it) at a shrewdly calculated 4.25 pm, when the patrons were mostly solitary and vaguely disgruntled males, a few enough to be individually aware of each other and surreptitiously absorbing every audible word even if they spoke none themselves. The first bartender recognized him as an obstreperous but lavish tipper, and greeted him with the perfect blend of obsequiousness and familiarity: "Hi, Tick. What's new today?"

"I dunno, Charlie. Gimme the usual—double."

"Yes, *sir*."

A quick and expert pouring and mixing.

"Y'know, Charlie, there are some guys in this world so stupid, I sometimes wonder how they ever learned to keep on breathing."

"I hear plenty of 'em gasping; but who did you have in mind?"

"Just a little while ago, I get in the damnedest argument with some thick-skulled bartender."

"You should stay out of those low-class bars, Tick."

"Yeah? Well, it all starts from talking about this place." Mr Way's voice was deliberately pitched to carry to all corners of the room, and it had the timbre of one who was not only unabashed by an audience but welcomed one. "Somehow this gets us on to astrology, see, which it seems this dope kind of goes for. So I'm only trying to show him how dumb he is. 'Look at it this way,' I tell him. 'There's only twelve signs to be born under, like there are twelve months in the year. But if you read those horoscopes, any day, they're the same for everybody born under the same sign. Now take any six guys sitting down to a poker game. You can bet two to one there'll be at least a couple of 'em born in the same month,' I says, 'but would you bet there'll always be a couple who'll have exactly the same luck and win or lose the same amount?' And you know what this jerk wants to argue about? Not about the intelligent reasoning I'm giving him. No. He wants to pick on my figures, and have it that it's only a fifty-fifty chance there'll be two guys born in the same month."

The bartender stayed where he was, polishing glasses. At that hour he had time to chat, before the feverish cocktail rush started, and Mr Way's obliquely insulting gambit had inevitably given him a controversial attitude towards a conversational subject that was already more intrinsically stimulating than most of the topics that get bandied across a bar.

"That doesn't sound so unreasonable, Tick. Let's see, if——"

"You want to take his side, Charlie, I'll save you the brain fever. 'People are getting born every day, all over the world,' says this moron. 'So there must be about the same number born every month. Now suppose you divide the year in half, six months to a half. You take six guys. Either they get born in one half or the other. So it's fifty-fifty.' . . . Now I ask you, Charlie, what sort of logic is that?"

"It makes a certain amount of sense," said the bartender stubbornly. "After all——"

Mr Way turned to the nearest listener, who had obviously been following the entire conversation, and offered him a smirking invitation to join the fun.

"Go on," he said. "Tell him that's why he'll be a bartender all his life."

"Okay, you tell me, Mr Jacobs," said the bartender defensively. "You're a good bridge player—how would *you* figure the odds in a deal like that?"

"I don't think your colleague was so stupid," said the newly appointed umpire deliberately. "He's just a fraction off. As I heard it, the condition was that two of these six men had to be born in the same month. Well, let's go with him up to a point, that five of them were born in five different months. You want to find the chances of the sixth man being born in one of those same five months. Well, anyone can see he's got five to choose from that'll do it; the other seven months of the year, he misses. So the exact odds are seven to five against him."

Mr Way regarded him with a baleful sneer.

"There must be something about bars that gets into people," he announced disgustedly. "Now I'll tell you the right and scientific answer. Any man's got the same chance of being born in one month as any other, hasn't he? So let's take any month—January. Give the first man a shot at it. Either he's born in January or he isn't. It can only be yes or no. Heads or tails. *There's* the fifty-fifty chance. Let's say he makes it. So give the second man a shot. Either he hits January or he misses. Heads or tails again. And the same for the third guy, and so on. So for these five guys in a row to all miss being born in January is like you tossing a coin and having it come down heads five times running. Sure, it can be done, but I'll bet two to one against it any time you want to play."

There was barely an instant's silence, sustained only by incredulous second-thinking, for nobody there was a mathematical prodigy; and then the first derisive retort became a fugue which became a chorus.

"You call *that* scientific?"

"Perhaps *I'm* stupid, but——"

"If *that's* what you mean by logic——"

"All right," retorted Mr Way, even more loudly and offensively. "Anyone who calls anyone else crazy should have the guts to back up his opinion. I'll back mine with good green money." He hauled out a roll of bills and slammed one on the counter. "I'll still lay ten bucks to five that out of any six men here, two were born in the same month."

The erstwhile referee sucked his cigar for a moment, and said slowly: "Well, if that's your attitude, and you want to pay ten to five *on* something that any fool can see should get you seven to five *against*, I guess I can bear to take it."

He was backed up by a respectable clamour of others who wanted a piece of this self-evident bonanza.

It was almost a classic example of the technique which had sustained Tick Way throughout his dubiously solvent life. First, the proposition to arouse the interest of a vast curious and inherently disputatious section of mankind, presented at a cold-bloodedly chosen hour when they would be most susceptible. Second, the channelling of their first thoughts into a fallacious pattern that they would soon adopt as their own, forgetting that he was the one who implanted it. Third, the presentation of a contrary theory so apparently absurd that the most mediocre intellect would reject it. And throughout and overall, a display of objectionable cockiness that was guaranteed to strangle the noblest impulse to show him his error kindly and disinterestedly.

For Mr Way was not one of those ingratiating swindlers who work on the softer side of their prey. The most brilliantly original facet of his art was in his development of a natural gift for making himself detestable. In a few scintillating minutes, he could inspire the mildest citizen with seductive thoughts of mayhem. But since he was too ludicrously puny for the average man to punch in the nose, most of them sublimated this healthy impulse into a willingness, indeed an eagerness, to take it out of his noisily proffered bankroll.

The fact that Simon Templar was not among the first of those who volunteered to fade him may have been due not so much to the Saint's mastery of theoretical figures as to his appreciation of live ones, and particularly the specimen who chose that moment to make her entrance.

It should be superfluous, after that sentence, for this chronicler to expatiate at much length upon the proportions and attractions of Hilda Mason, which in cold truth were not intrinsically different from those of any other girl who gets herself into these stories. They were, however, striking enough for him to have judged her at once to be the most interesting girl on the Interplanetary Hotel beach on the first day he cased it, with an outstanding chance of defending that title against all comers from plenty of other beaches and for quite a few orbits. Let it be on the record that she had light brown hair and light brown eyes and was almost criminally young and glowing, and that the puffy balding-grey man with her who looked easily old enough to be her father proved on investigation to be her father—a phenomenon which in Miami Beach in the season was not merely epochal but had also made the Saint's casual campaign almost effortless.

"I'm not late, am I?" she said.

"Not one second," he smiled. "And I'd allowed for half an hour. Which gives us time for just one family-style drink together."

"I accept with pleasure," said her father, sinking into another chair. "But I assure you, that's as long as you'll be stuck with me. I only came this far to keep Hilda company in case you happened to be late. I brought her up according to the old-fashioned doctrine that punctuality is the most inexpensive of grand gestures; but one can't count on everyone else having the same philosophy."

Simon ordered the drinks from a waiter who was already waiting, fortunately, for more customers were beginning to seep in. But the room was still populated sparsely enough for Mr Way's discordantly jeering voice to snag the attention of the newcomers as it rose in raucous triumph a few minutes later.

"October! Here's another guy born in October! And he's only Number Five. Now who says I didn't prove my point?"

"What is this all about?" George Mason asked.

Simon gave him a factual synopsis, untrimmed with any personal comment, and Mason shook his head.

"The man must be out of his mind. Or else he's got money to burn and he'd rather burn it than admit he's wrong."

The group that was gravitating towards the noise focus of the bar evidently shared this opinion, and furthermore had no scruples about taking advantage of either contingency. Nor were they discouraged by the accident that had cost them a few dollars on the first sampling of nativities.

"Any fool can be lucky," growled the good bridge player who had been finessed into becoming spokesman for the opposition. "But that doesn't prove he's right. If you want to convince me the odds are what you say, you'd have to win two out of three times. With six total strangers."

"You think you aren't strangers?" squawked Mr Way.

"You think one of you is my stooge? I'd really hate to have such a dishonest mind as to even think that. Or to be such a bad loser as to say it. But don't make any cracks about backing down until we see who's doing it. You want to try this again twice more, or two hundred times, I'll give you the same odds."

"There aren't that many people here——"

"Then we go out and ask any six guys in the street. And you pick 'em. Or easier still, we send out to the office for something like *Who's Who*—they must have a copy in a joint like this. You name any six names, so long as they aren't *your* ancestors. Or shut your eyes and pick 'em with a pin. Just show me the colour of your money first!"

The debate progressed without any diminution of temperature towards the next inevitable showdown.

"If I'd known bars were such fun," Hilda said, "I'd have lied about my age long before this."

"You probably did, anyhow," said her father tolerantly. "Only you were afraid to try it on the fancy places, which are much less willing to be fooled than certain others, I'm told."

"I wonder who told you."

The Saint grinned.

"I must hear more about this, George," he murmured. "Some time when the child isn't fanning us with its big shell-pink ears. Right now, I honestly hate to drink and run, but we're stuck with the programme I sold her. At this hour, it'll be mostly a crawl down to the very end of the Beach for Joe's immortal stone crabs. And from there, it's another long haul over to Coral Gables and this show she wanted to see. Until the millennium when it dawns on theatrical producers that an eight-fifteen curtain is the ideal time to ensure a hostile and dyspeptic reception from anyone who also likes a nice peaceful dinner——"

"Don't worry about me, my boy," said Mr Mason expansively. "I shall stay here for a little while and improve my education."

"Just don't pay any padded tuition fees," said the Saint frivolously.

It was not until after he had ordered their stone crabs at Joe's with a bottle of Willm Gewurtztraminer, and they were toying with cigarettes and Dry Sack while they waited, that he realized that he might have been a little too flippant.

"I only hope Papa doesn't get into anything silly," Hilda said.

"Is he likely to?" asked the Saint. "He seems a long way from being senile, to me."

"He does like a little gamble, though. And he can't forget that he was an insurance company statistician for thirty years. Of course that's only a glorified kind of book-keeping, but he sometimes thinks it makes him an authority on anything to do with figures. He might have a hard time staying out of that argument in the bar."

"That shouldn't get him in any serious trouble. . . . Well, I admit I hadn't thought of it that way. It sounded like a typical bar-room argument, with nobody really knowing the score. They were all talking through their hats, I may tell you. Let's find out what the odds really are."

He turned a menu over, took out a ball-point pen, and began jotting.

"Do you really know how to work it out?" she asked.

"I don't let on to everyone, but I had one of those dreary old out-dated educations. Lots of gruesomely hard study, and no credits at all for football, fretwork, or folk dancing. But I think I can figure it the text-book way."

"You'll have to tell me. I even flunked Domestic Science."

"They must have tested you in the wrong domicile. But

this is how you have to look at it. The first guy can be born in any month, as somebody said. When were you born?"

"April."

"Okay. Then the second guy has eleven months to choose from, that'll lose for Loud Mouth back there."

"That sounds right."

"So the second guy was born in May. Now up comes the third guy. He has two months to dodge, out of twelve. On any of the other ten, he still wins from Loud Mouth."

"Even I can follow that. So it leaves the fourth man nine months, and the fifth man eight months, and the sixth man seven months. But——"

"Now according to the Law of Probabilities in my school book, and don't ask me who made it or why it works that way, to find the odds against all those things happening in succession, you don't add them up, you have to multiply them. Like this."

He had written:

$$\frac{11}{12} \times \frac{10}{12} \times \frac{9}{12} \times \frac{8}{12} \times \frac{7}{12}$$

"Don't forget that eight-fifteen curtain," Hilda said.

"It's not so hard as all that."

He made a few quick cross-cancellations to simplify the problem, did a little rapid arithmetic, and ended up with the fraction:

$$\frac{385}{1728}$$

"That's fine," she said. "But how does it give you the odds?"

"It means that theoretically, out of any 1728 batches of six people, there should only be 385 batches in which two of 'em *weren't* born in the same month—meaning where Loud Mouth would lose his bet. 385 from 1728 leaves 1343. So the odds are 1343 to 385, which——"

The Saint made another swift calculation, and whistled.

"It comes out at almost three-and-a-half to one," he concluded. "And everybody thought Loud Mouth was nuts to be offering two to one—only a bit more than half the honest odds! A fellow could make a career out of being so crazy!"

Her face fell for a moment, in transparent anxiety, before she forced herself to suppress the thought.

"Well, after all, it's not so different from the kind of statistics that insurance companies worry about, is it? Papa probably knows the correct way to work it out, just like you did."

"I hope so," said the Saint; but for the rest of the evening only the superficial part of his attention was completely available to the conversation, the entertainment, or even the notable charms of his companion.

Now that he had belatedly been obliged to think seriously about it, his fateful instinct for chicanery and the fast double-shuffle could recognize the loud and unlovable gamecock of the Interplanetary Hotel's Spaceship Room as a probable charter member of an ancient fraternity, with a new angle. But the most interesting novelty was not the switch from the stereotyped con man's beguiling suaveness to Mr Way's crude art of alienation, but the upper-class mathematics on which the nasty little man had based his act. This was an artifice that Simon Templar had never met before, and he seriously wondered if it might not prove too tricky even for him.

He had even graver doubts when he saw the obnoxious operator again the next day. Wandering up to the Futuramic Terrace in search of a long cooling potion after a couple of hours of swimming and sunning himself on the beach, he spotted the little man sitting at one of the tables by the pool, unselfconsciously exposing as much of his bulbously misproportioned physique as could not be contained in a pair of garishly flowered Hawaiian shorts, and holding forth to a pimpled and sulky-mouthed young man and two tough-looking middle-aged women with the unmistakable air of dames who had never yet lost an elbowing contest at a bargain counter.

The table, like all others on the terrace, sported a cloth patterned in red, white, and blue stripes about three inches wide; and Mr Way was flipping cigarettes a foot or two into the air so that they fell on it at various random angles.

"In Pakistan, where it's practically the national game, they call it Tiger Toss—from the board they play on, which has black and yellow stripes. And they use carved ivory sticks instead of cigarettes. But the measurements are relatively just the same : the sticks are exactly as long as the stripes are wide. Like on this cloth, the stripes happen to be just as wide as one of these cigarettes is long. See?"

He demonstrated.

"Then you toss a stick, or a cigarette, on to the board, or the cloth, and see how it lands. It has to spin in the air and turn over so that there's no chance of controlling it. If it comes down completely inside a stripe, you win. If it falls across a dividing line, you lose. Like this. . . . But wait till you hear the catch."

The Saint waited, at a diffident distance towards the background, but no farther off than other patrons or passers-by whose attention had been caught and held by Mr Way's provocatively high-decibel style of conversation.

"The pitch they give the peasants is that this is the rajah's way of distributing charity so as to do the most good. You know—if you give a rupee to every starving slob, they'll all be just as hungry again tomorrow; but playing Tiger Toss, the lucky ones could make a pot of money. And the guy who's running the game—who's got a concession from the rajah, of course—show's 'em how easy it is. 'Look,' he says, 'even if a stick falls at right angles to the pattern, there's still room for it inside a stripe. And the more it falls at an angle, the more room there is.'" Mr Way illustrated the fact with a cigarette. "'Until if it was parallel with the stripes, there'd be room for eight or nine of 'em to lie in there side by side without touching the dividing line,' says this official gypper. But they never got me to play. No, sir." Mr Way's insufferably malevolent stare swung around him like a scythe. "Before I'd buy a tale about a philanthropic rajah, I'll believe in a big-hearted Shylock."

Without giving anybody time to draw a deep breath, he picked up another cigarette and went on : "Right away, *I* can see how anybody with a grain of sense would look at it. Either the stick gotta fall at right angles to the stripes—like this—or it doesn't. It's as simple as that. One or the other. A fifty-fifty chance. And once it falls like this, square across the stripe, if it's only a hair off dead centre, see, it has to touch the line or cross over the next stripe. Now, there's so little chance it'll fall dead centre, one in a million maybe—you can forget it. So it still boils down to whether it falls square or not."

"Now wait a minute, smarty-pants," riposted one of the women, in an almost equally strident voice. "If that's what you call using a grain of sense, saying it's fifty-fifty if it falls this way or two hundred other ways——"

"At least, there are ninety degrees in a right angle," corrected the pouty young man. "So if you said eighty-nine other——"

"Are you ribbing me, trying to sound like those other benighted heathens?" snarled Mr Way. "Or if that's what you call your intelligent opinion, would you back it up with any more than hot air?" Even from his attenuated costume he was able to produce a wad of currency which he slammed on the table with a vehemence that almost equalled a slap in the face. "You want to bet even money with me? I'll say the cigarette touches the line, you can do the tossing, and we'll see who comes out ahead. And I'll fade anyone else who wants to come in."

Simon adroitly evaded the contentious bantam's challenging eye, and drifted on to find himself a vacant table, where he asked a mildly befogged waiter for a Pimm's Cup, a pencil, and a piece of paper. When all these items were finally delivered, he sipped the cold ambrosial drink and went soberly to work with the other articles. By that time, a "Tiger Toss" school was in full and audible session on the other side of the terrace, with Mr Way the self-appointed banker daring all and sundry to prove themselves as ignorant as the credulous Pakistanis.

The techniques of bogus backgrounding, Machiavellian misdirection, and a gadfly approach that could be relied on to make almost anyone but a lower-case saint too furious to think straight, were the same as the night before. But the specific probability problem, shorn of the artistic camouflage, Simon soon found, would be unscientifically called a snorter.

Since it is not the purpose of this story to double as a first primer of higher mathematics, which it may already have started to sound like, the reasoning by which the Saint solved this rather interesting equation must be omitted from the present text. To anyone who has not set at least one foot in the mystic realm of trigonometry it would be meaningless. Those who have studied such subjects, of course, may recognize it at once under the name of Buffon's Problem. The Saint took much longer to wring the correct answer out of his rusty recollections, and when he had done it he had even more respect for the perverse astuteness of Mr Way.

It was quite comforting to persuade himself that such comparatively small-time improbity was not worthy of his serious attention, and that the types who paid Mr Way for improving their education would not be mortally hurt by the fees; but this consolation was short-lived. Chronologically, it lasted about two minutes, until his reverie was cut short by Hilda Mason's voice beside him.

"Well, here's the man who knows his arithmetic."

Simon turned and jumped up, grinning.

"I was starting to worry about you, not seeing you on the beach all morning. I was afraid I'd shown you one night club too many."

"I did sleep a bit late. . . . And then, Papa and I had a lot to talk about when I got up."

George Mason was with her, in a gaily checkered terry-cloth robe that failed to obscure a certain haggardness in his amiably inflated presence.

"Like a dutiful daughter, she is understating the fact that I made a fool of myself last night," he said, lowering himself into the next seat. "After you left me, I was inveigled into expressing my views on that birthday bet. Unfortunately, my reasoning seems to have been erroneous. Hilda has been telling me how you worked it out, which I now remember is the proper method—but I'm afraid this is a little late. Somehow I managed to lose almost two hundred dollars to Mr Way on various names chosen at random from *Who's Who* and other directories. And then, somehow, we began playing this game of Tiger Toss, which I see he is still at."

The girl glanced across the terrace, and down again to the scratch-pad on which Simon had been trying his creaky computations.

"Were you just working that one out?" she asked.

"Yes. And I have a headache which only another Pimm's will cure."

"Tell us the answer."

"I can do that, but don't ask me to explain it. It's a bit more complicated than the birthday deal. If you don't want to be bludgeoned with a lot of double-talk about sine curves and spandrels, you'll have to take my word for it that the theoretical odds are almost exactly seven to four against the stick, or the cigarette, falling cleanly inside a stripe."

There was the kind of silence which is tritely called pregnant.

"And I was playing him for even money," Mason said sombrely. "It honestly looked like an even bet to me, because . . . Well, my stupid reasons aren't very important, are they? However, they cost me another hundred and fifty dollars. And by that time, I had imbibed a trifle more than I'm used to—enough, I fear, to make me somewhat reckless. When he offered to let me match him double or quits, in some simple variation he calls Monte Carlo Match, I was optimistic enough to accept. As a result, I may not be much wiser, but I am some seven hundred dollars poorer."

"And so," Hilda said, "this is our last day here."

She was much too young to show the same grey deflation as her father, but young enough for an excessive brightness of eye to be betrayed by a slight unsteadiness of lip.

"Does it make all that difference?" Simon asked.

"It does to us. You see, we're not quite like the usual people who come to these places. With a job like his, and a family to bring up, Papa could never afford it. But he always promised me that when all the others were safely on their own—I'm the youngest—and the time came for him to retire, we'd have one tremendous splurge and see what it felt like to be millionaires for a couple of weeks. And I held him to it; although I've got a secretarial job now and I'll pay him back for my share eventually. I thought he should have it for once in his life, before he settles down to scraping along on his pension. But we don't really belong here, and since this has happened we've got to be sensible."

"Don't feel sorry for me," said the older man defiantly. "Things like this have happened to millionaires, too. And I am still not so broke that I can't insist on you being my guest for lunch."

The Saint nodded slowly.

"No millionaire could do more, George."

"There's nothing else we *can* do, is there?" Hilda asked wistfully.

"Not legally," Simon said. "You haven't been swindled —technically. Nobody sold you the MacArthur Causeway, or a submerged piece of real estate. You could accuse someone of cheating at cards, but how would you accuse them of cheating at figures, the way Loud Mouth does it? A difference of opinion is what makes bets; and how would you convince a cop who has to do his own arithmetic on his fingers that Loud Mouth is taking an unfair advantage? And even if you could charge him with illegal gambling, you wouldn't get any bounty on his hide. All you can do is remember that you were taken by one of the most original artists I've come across for a long time, if that makes you feel any better. And don't look at me with those big fawn eyes, Hilda, because I'm on vacation, too."

But although she instantly stopped looking at him like that, he knew that his protestation was as hollow as it had always been, since the very first time he had tried to stick to it.

He also wished he could stop being stuck with such preposterous projects. For the one thing that he had been most solidly convinced of by his strenuous figuring was that in any straight mathematical tussle with the talented Mr Way he would have about the same prospects as a rheumatic water buffalo in a greyhound race.

He thought that if there were laws against wicked old men taking advantage of trusting young girls, there should also be laws against young girls *and* old men trusting merely middle-aged bandits to rescue them from grades of wickedness that a college professor might have been puzzled to cope with.

In spite of which, and with no obtrusive sign of having racked his brain and paced his room for two hours in search of an answer, he was in the Spaceship Room again before four-thirty, ensconced at a strategic corner table that was still within easy speaking distance of the bar. From there he espied Mr Way's blustery approach from the lobby; and by the time the percentage player strutted in, he was intensely absorbed in an eye-catching experiment.

On the table-top, he had laid out three ordinary poker chips. These he was shuffling around into various small patterns, sometimes turning one over and rearranging them, occasionally closing his eyes and fumbling for one at random, and turning it over and staring at it and finally shuffling the pattern again. All of this was done with a scowl of agonized concentration, and an air of frustrated bafflement, which were an almost deafening invitation to any other solitary customer in need of a conversational gambit.

Tick Way, with a hypertrophied affinity for brain-teasers to augment his common human curiosity, resisted the bait perhaps 39·65% less seconds than an average target might have held out. Thus he was comfortably ahead of anyone else to turn from his bar stool, after he had been served, and baldly accept the hook.

"What in hell," he demanded, with his distinctive kind of bumptious bonhomie, "are you playing at, buddy?"

"I'm glad you asked me that . . . chum," said the Saint, without even regurgitating. "You might be able to help me work this out. I've heard you talking about this sort of thing a couple of times, and it sounded to me as if you knew more about figures than most people."

"I probably do," admitted Mr Way, with the most affability he was capable of. "What's bothering you?"

"It's this silly game," said the Saint. "A chap showed it to me in the club car, on the train coming down here. He told me it was something the rich mandarins used to play in China, for concubines—Dong Hai, or something like that, he called it. You're supposed to have three plaques like this, all exactly the same. One of them has some Chinese character painted on both sides. The second has the identical character on one side only. And the third is blank on both sides. Instead of Chinese characters, we just made an X with a pencil, the way I've marked these."

The connoisseur of hazards was already moving over to the table.

"Okay, what's the game?"

"Well, you drop the three chips into a bag, or a box—or a hat." Simon did that. "You shake 'em up under the table, where nobody can see what happens to them. Then if it's your turn, you pick out any one of 'em without looking. Go on, you try it. You take it out and slam it on the table, so that anyone can see what's on the top side —whether it's marked or not—but nobody knows what's on the under side. Then you try to guess what's underneath, an X or nothing."

Mr Way thoughtfully turned over the chip he had put down. Simon spilled out the other two beside it. The little man picked them up and examined them. A newcomer would have wondered why anyone ever called him Loud Mouth.

"Here's how this chap explained it to me," said the Saint, reaching for his pen and a handy piece of ash-tray advertising. "And it might help you to visualize it quicker. Let's pretend we can see both sides of these chips at once. I'll draw both sides of each chip and tie them together. Here's the one with a cross on both sides, for a start. . . ."

He drew it, followed by two similarly attenuated dumbbells.

". . . and the one with a cross on one side only, and the double-blank. Now, as this chap says first, anyone can see there are three crosses and three blanks, altogether, so if you just shut your eyes and guessed what side was down— or up, for that matter—you'd have an even chance."

"Yeah, if you're guessing——"

"But suppose you're looking. Suppose the chip on the table shows a cross. Then you know it can only be one of these first two, don't you? In other words, the under side is either a cross—or a blank. An even chance. . . . On the other hand, if the side that's up is blank, you know the chip must be one of these second two. So the bottom either has a cross—or it doesn't. Again, it's fifty-fifty. Or it *seems* to be."

"What d'ya mean, it *seems*?"

"Well, that's what was bothering me. Because when I was doing the guessing, I was right about half the time. But this other chap guessed right much more often than not. I lost quite a packet playing with him. So I've started wondering if I was unlucky, or whether there's some trick to it that I haven't seen. I'm sure that the crosses were all exactly alike, and there was nothing on the chips that you could find by feeling them—I thought of that. And the way we played, he couldn't have done any sleight of hand. But if it's legitimate, why go through such a complicated business to set up an even chance?"

Mr Way fiddled with the chips and frowned over the diagram for a full minute, which is quite a long pause in a conversation. And if his had been an electronic brain instead of the old-fashioned variety, one would have sworn that one could feel the churning incandescence of his tubes.

It had been manifest from the start, to his practically singleminded instincts, that some deceit was involved. But the same ingenuous presentation which had caught his interest had also effectively nipped off any branch lines of thought which might have led towards mechanical props or common legerdemain. He knew that he was confronting some subtle trick of skilful misdirection from the same family as those which had long provided him with a fairly painless livelihood, but a trick which he had somehow failed to master before. It had given him a twinge of professional jealousy to discover that some cheesy plagiarist must be exploiting a colourable imitation of his own method in positively overlapping territory; but this pang had been rapidly alleviated by more constructive thoughts of the profits he might derive from swiping this Dong Hai routine for his own repertoire. All he needed was to twig the trick, and he even had a self-confessed pushover already set up and waiting for the shove.

It may be cited as some kind of testimonial to his misguided genius that he found the solution in those sixty seconds of seething cogitation—a par for the problem which only the most razor-witted reader is likely to have equalled, although in this case no abstruse mathematics whatever were involved. Perhaps it was only the gigantic blatancy of the logical pitfall that made it so hard for a devious mind to see.

But when it did dawn on him like a blast of lightning, it was purely to the credit of Mr Way's personal discipline that he did not emit a screech of triumph like the orgasm of a banshee, or even exhibit the faintest furtive smugness. He merely wagged his head, with a disillusioned and contemptuous weariness.

"There's nothing wrong with the game, bud," he said. "The only thing wrong is that some bum sports always think they've been robbed if they don't win."

"But why go to all that trouble to invent a game like that when you might as well flip a coin?"

"Don't ask me, my friend. Maybe these mandarins were too rich to carry small change. Maybe the concubines would've been offended about being flipped for. Maybe they got bored with flipping coins and had to think up something different. How do any betting games get started?"

"But an even chance——"

"What's more complicated than a roulette table? And yet half the people you see in a casino are playing the even chances—red and black, odds and evens, high and low. It just seems more glamorous, or something, to do it that way. I could get bored with tossing heads and tails myself. I'm a sucker for a new game. Why don't we try this one? This time, you might be lucky. That'd prove it was on the level."

"I could use a bit of luck," Simon grumbled, declining the gibe. "How much d'you want to play for? Would five bucks be too high for you?"

"I thought you told me you'd lost a *packet*," sneered

Mr Way. "How long did it take you, at those prices? Or how much do you call a packet? Most times, I'd say that any bet less than a ten-spot wasn't worth the effort; but if you're strapped——"

"Okay," said the Saint. "Make it ten dollars."

He scraped the chips into his hat and shook it under the table.

"Who goes first?"

"After you," said Mr Way.

Simon brought out a chip and slapped it down. When he took his hand off it, it revealed a pencilled X.

"Blank," said the Saint, and turned it over.

The other side was blank. Mr Way pulled out his roll, peeled off a bill, and handed it over. Simon threw the chip back in his hat and passed it to Mr Way under the table. Mr Way took out a chip, laid it down, and exposed a cross.

"Another cross," he said, turning it over.

He was wrong. The other side was blank again.

On the next draw, Simon showed a blank, called for a cross, but turned up another blank. Mr Way also picked a blank, called it blanks back-to-back, and lost—when the chip was turned over, it showed an X on the other side.

Mr Way paid off with equanimity. He was betting on a cast-iron percentage, and he could afford to wait for the dividends.

Several plays and some three hundred dollars later he was still waiting. He had won a few times, but not nearly so often as his opponent. That was when, convinced that the laws of probability could not be defied indefinitely, he made the utterly amateurish mistake of suggesting that they should double the stakes to speed up the action.

The Saint let himself be cajoled and insulted into that

with the most irritating reluctance, and had soon taken another five hundred and forty dollars of Mr Way's cash. They doubled the stakes again, and Simon won another forty dollars on his correct guess and another forty on the little man's incorrect one.

"This can get damn monotonous, after all," Mr Way conceded. "Let's try some other game."

"But I'm just getting lucky at this one," Simon protested. "Don't be discouraged because I'm having a winning streak. Let me have my fun. It probably won't last long."

Mr Way thumbed through the very thin sheaf of currency that was still left to him.

"You'll have to take my cheque, then. I don't have any more folding stuff on me——"

"I'm terribly sorry, dear boy," said the Saint earnestly. "But that's against the vow I made to my dear old grandmother on her death-bed. I can see her now, with the setting sun lighting up her nose, and her poor tired trembling fingers hardly able to hold on to the gin bottle. 'Promise me,' she burped, 'that whatever the bet is, you'll never take any chiselling bastard's IOU. Always make 'em lay it on the line, son,' she said, and——"

"I'm just wondering," snarled Mr Way, "if I should have another look at those chips."

"Help yourself," said the Saint aggrievedly. "But don't forget you were the one who said that some bum sports always think they've been robbed if they don't win."

What Tick Way had to contribute to the remainder of the debate is perhaps largely unsuited to verbatim quotation.

"But how did you *do* it?" pleaded Hilda Mason.

"I simply conned him into playing strictly by the odds,"

said the Saint. "With a mentality like his, he was wide open."

"I am probably nearing my dotage," George Mason said, "but I still don't see the catch."

Simon reproduced the diagram he had drawn for Mr Way.

"It's built right into the rules. As you see, there are two chips which you might call 'doubles'—that is, if there's an X on one side there's an X on the other, or if it's blank on one side it's blank on the other. There's only one chip that has two different sides. Now the three chips are thrown into a hat and one is drawn at random. Therefore the odds are two to one that it'll be a 'double.' So if you see a cross, you call a cross; and if you see a blank you call a blank; and two out of three times you'll win. What you have to think of isn't the chance of what *could* be on the other side, but the odds on *which chip has been drawn.* Your pal Tick was sharp enough to spot that."

"Then why did he lose?"

"Because I cheated," said the Saint proudly. "I changed the odds. Since he relies on his gift for figures instead of manual dexterity, I thought he might have a blind spot for physical hanky-panky—which I'm rather good at. I made him a bit blinder with his own technique of misdirection, rubbing it in about how there couldn't be any funny juggling. But I was palming an extra chip with a cross on one side and blank on the other. I rung that in, so that there were two of that kind, and took out one of the doubles. Sometimes I changed them back, so he wouldn't notice that there was one double that never showed up. But most of the time, the odds were the exact opposite of what he was counting on." Simon began to peel layers off a thick bundle of green paper. "Now, it was about seven hundred dollars you lost, wasn't it?"

"But we can't take that," Hilda objected, half laughing and half crying.

"Why not? It's your money, isn't it? And I made a small profit for myself. Besides, I only did it because I couldn't let you pack up and go home before we got to know each other a lot better," said the Saint.

The Water Merchant

"I'll tell you what I think of Foreign Aid," said the Saint, thoughtfully twisting the newspaper into the semblance of a short rope. "I think that if the Commies had assigned their best brains to inventing a gimmick that'd bleed America like a built-in leak in the economy, they couldn't have come up with anything cleverer."

"I don't know about that," Howard Mayne said. "But——"

"It saddles the poor squirming US taxpayer with an annual bill of billions of dollars, for which he gets nothing but jobs for the gaggle of bureaucrats who administer it."

"Perhaps; but——"

"The more advanced countries simply hate him a bit more, down inside, the way all proud people who are down on their luck react to being charity cases. The more backward ones simply insist more loudly that there must be no strings attached—which means that *their* bureaucrats want no check on how much of the gravy they can siphon off into their own pockets, while they personally take all the credit for what little trickles through to the populace, which is probably still out throwing rotten eggs at American ambassadors."

"You'd better not let any *Daily Worker* correspondent hear you. He'd discover that you were an imperialist, colonialist——"

"I damn well am an imperialist colonialist," Simon Templar agreed, warming to his subject. "I think the old British Empire, on the whole, was one of the best things this world has ever known. The good old colonialist went out into the wilderness and tamed a lot of unsanitary savages, brought them down out of trees or up out of mud huts, taught them to wash themselves and stop eating their elderly relatives for dinner, and with a few exceptions left them a hell of a lot better off than they would have made themselves in another three centuries, just in exchange for exploiting some natural resources that the benighted heathen didn't know what to do with anyhow. So all they get for it is a lot of abuse, mostly from characters who wouldn't know how to spell the word if it wasn't for the education the wicked imperialists crammed into them. I think it's an everlasting pity that more Englishmen didn't have the guts to stand up and trumpet the facts, instead of being hustled into dropping their colonies like naughty boys caught with a fistful of stolen candy—by a lot of bloody-handed Russians, and sanctimonious Americans firmly settled in one of the biggest countries ever swiped from its aborigines."

"You may be right," Mayne said placatingly. "But I was talking about a matter of Domestic Aid. Just because I mentioned that there was some phoney-sounding Arab in the background shouldn't get us off on all these tangents."

With his pleasantly ugly face and competent air, he looked like the very personification of the idealized detective familiar to every television watcher, and the fact that he was not playing such a part every week for a network sponsor was a commentary on the unpredictable hazards of acting as a profession rather than on his personal talent.

Mrs Sophie Yarmouth, his aunt, a determined woman who was also present, chimed in more forcefully : "Howard is right, Mr Templar. You're only trying to dodge the issue. You set yourself up once as a guardian of society against racketeers and swindlers, so you have a duty to do something about them whenever a case is laid in your lap.

Just as you did when you cleared up that affair that I got involved in."

Because of his friendship with Howard Mayne, the Saint had once recouped a ten thousand dollar investment that Mrs Yarmouth had once made with a good bunco artist, as has been recounted elsewhere in these chronicles. When he had phoned Mayne on this subsequent transit through Los Angeles, however, it had only been to invite himself for a sociable drink, with no suspicion that he might be drafted to bring succour to another sucker. But such inflictions were among the occupational overhead of the life he had chosen for himself, and sometimes they had to be accepted.

"Okay," he said resignedly. "I'll drop in on your poor relations from Texas on my way through La Jolla. Although trying to save an oil tycoon from being taken for a few grand, even if this proposition he's interested in *is* a swindle, strikes me as almost as important a project as sending Foreign Aid to some Persian-Gulf Poobah who's having trouble meeting the tab for a hundred-girl harem."

Walt Jobyn, to do him justice even at the expense of flattery, could never have been seriously compared with the lord of a hundred-girl harem. He had quite enough to cope with in the person of his one lawful wedded wife, Felicity, a lady of Amazonian build and an equivalently positive personality, whose affectionate concern for his welfare had an intensity that might have made a strong man quail.

Mr Jobyn was not built on this heroic scale, having been a lean and often hungry cowboy until the barren section on which he was raising a few head of hamburger cattle had found itself in the very centre of a circumference of deep holes which had been bored by an exploding contingent of oil-sniffing geologists. The fees he had been able to exact for letting other similar perforations be made in his land had thereafter relieved him of all financial problems other than those of making tax returns and finding ways to invest a residue which was still more than a spouse with unlimited charge accounts could spend.

In spite of these frightful burdens, Mr Jobyn had not changed very much except in such superficial details as having cleaner fingernails and a wardrobe by Neiman-Marcus instead of Levi Strauss, and his reception of the Saint was as heartily hospitable as if he had been home on the range instead of in the lobby of the fanciest hotel in La Jolla, that self-styled jewel of the Southern California coast some ten miles above San Diego.

"I sure am glad to see yuh," he said, giving Simon a powerful bony handshake. "I've read so much about yuh, I feel like I'd knowed yuh ever since I was a boy. And yet yuh don't look that old."

"I cheat," said the Saint. "I take things like vitamins and exercise. And I'm too stupid to worry, which is what makes dignified grey hair and distinguished wrinkles."

"Yuh look mighty good to me," Jobyn said. "I wish I was stupid like you. Or Felicity didn't think she was so smart. I'm hopin' yuh'll be able to straighten her out about this investment I'm thinkin' of makin'. She's been goin' on at me so hard, I declare yuh might think I was figurin' on buyin' into a bawdyhouse instead of a legitimate business."

They perched on stools at the bar, and Simon accepted a Peter Dawson. Jobyn tasted a straight shot and told the bartender to leave them the bottle.

"Yes, sir," he said, "anyone 'ud think I wasn't bright enough to spot a wooden nickel if it had termites crawlin' all over it."

"You sound very sure that this business *is* legitimate," Simon said.

"O' course I'm sure," Jobyn said pettishly. "Otherwise

I wouldn't be figurin' on buyin' into it. Ain't nobody told yuh nothin' about it?"

"All I know is that Mrs Yarmouth said you were on the point of being taken for a small fortune by some faker who claims to be able to get fresh water from the sea."

"That's the way Sophie *would* put it. She's on Felicity's side, naturally, being as they're cousins. And if Felicity had her way about it, there wouldn't be any satellites goin' around the earth, because she'd've called anyone who said he could send a rocket into space a faker, just because nobody ever done it before. You wait till yuh meet Doc Nemford. You'll see for yuhself he's a real serious scientific fella."

Felicity Jobyn, whom Simon met at lunch, had her own version of this.

"The only serious science he knows," she stated categorically, "is how to part a fool from his money."

"Now, why do yuh keep sayin' that, Felicity?" protested the tycoon plaintively. "You've seen him yuhself, pumpin' sea water through this machine of his, an' it comin' out sweet as a mountain spring, just as fast as he puts it in."

"I've seen it but I still don't believe it, like I've seen a magician saw a woman in half."

"It isn't altogether impossible—this water business, I mean," Simon ventured. "They already know quite a few ways of doing it. But so far they haven't been able to make one cheap enough to be commercially attractive."

"And they aren't likely to," Mrs Jobyn said crisply. "It's against Nature, that's all."

If the Saint had been President, he would have appointed her ambassador to Moscow. No mere second-generation disciple of Stalin would have put anything over on her.

"You're probably right," he said diplomatically. "But I

have met a few crackpot inventors who actually invented something. I'd like to see this trick for myself."

"You do that," said Mrs Jobyn, "and then tell Walt how it's done. Maybe that'll get some sense into his stubborn head."

The mother of Mr Nemford, for such reasons as motivate parents, had had him christened with the name of Stanley, but that was a fact which he revealed only to such tiresome officials as insisted on a meticulous filling out of forms. To everyone else, even in his teens, he had never been anything but "Doc"—a cognomen which fitted him like the proverbial glove, and which had pointed the way to an almost predestined career from the first time he had studied himself analytically in a mirror. With the congenital advantages of intense deep-set eyes sandwiched between a bulging forehead and ascetically hollow cheeks leading to a thin artistic jaw, even before he was old enough to vote he had looked more like a doctor of something highly intellectual than most men who had worked for years to earn the title.

The house where he was living in the vicinity of Mission Beach, about six miles south of La Jolla, was perfectly appropriate for an unworldly scientist or a struggling inventor. "Cottage" would have been a determined salesman's word for it, but "shack" would have been a description more realistic than real estate agents professionally care to be. In those days there was still a considerable colony of such clapboard shanties clustered around the lagoon which the coast road skirted on the west and the main highway to San Diego evaded inland, doomed soon to be mowed down by the inexorable march of building-code suburban progress, but surviving for a little while as one of the last relics of a more picturesque and carefree pre-boom and pre-industrial California which even a man without a grey hair on his head might remember as a dim once-upon-a-time.

From Doc Nemford's point of view, its greatest asset, far outweighing the draughty windows, antique plumbing, and incredibly shabby furniture, was its private pier, which projected some forty feet out into the lagoon from his narrow frontage on the water. Some much earlier landlord or tenant had created it by pile-driving lengths of three-inch pipe into the bottom of the shallow bay until they stood firm, connecting them with elbows and other threaded lengths of galvanized pipe, and overlaying this framework with a series of occasionally horizontal planks. The resultant structure might not have met any conventional engineering specifications, but it did provide a platform on which a number of reasonably sized and careful people could walk out a little way over the tidal waters of the inlet.

Simon Templar was one of a small party who did this that afternoon, in the train of Doc Nemford, who was trundling his contrivance in front of him on an ordinary garden wheelbarrow. The other members of the equipage were Walt Jobyn, who had presented the Saint as a possible partner in his investment, and the Arab emissary who had sparked the Saint's diatribe on the subject of Foreign Aid merely by being mentioned, a Colonel Hamzah.

Hamzah was a short but portly man with crinkly black hair, an enormous nose, and teeth as big as piano ivories, some of which were likewise black. He had said "How do you do?" when he was introduced, and therewith seemed to have exhausted his vocabulary; but to every other remark that was addressed to him, and some that were not, he responded with a vast if noncommittal display of his keyboard incisors.

Doc Nemford, however, had welcomed the Saint with

an amiable vagueness that went well with his scholarly mien, and revealed no trace of guilt or apprehension. In the Saint's ruthless system of reasoning, this still left open the possibilities that Nemford was a consummate actor, or that he was one of an increasingly rarer breed of innocents to whom the name of Simon Templar did not immediately evoke "The Robin Hood of Modern Crime" as an almost liturgical response. But he had betrayed no reluctance whatever to the proposal that he should give another demonstration of his process.

"Colonel Hamzah had asked me to let him make another quantity test, in any case," he said. "I'm sure he won't mind if you watch it."

Hamzah had presumably acquiesced with one of his dental exposures.

"What principle are you working on?" Simon inquired.

"The elementary principle that water is basically a simple liquid, and anything you put into it you should be able to take out," Nemford said indulgently. "If the thing was a lump of iron, you'd say that was obvious. Well, a sodium molecule isn't fundamentally different, it's only very much smaller."

"Does that mean it should be as easy as getting the eggs back out of an omelette?" asked the Saint ingenuously.

"That isn't quite the same," Nemford replied with unruffled patience. "Nobody has ever claimed to be able to do that. But everyone knows at least one way to get fresh water from the sea. By evaporation, for instance. Of course, that's much too slow to be efficient on a large scale. There are other ways—ion exchange and so forth —but they're quite expensive, too, even with atomic power. So I won't waste time trying to explain them. My method is completely different, anyhow."

"And what *is* your method, Doc?"

"It would be quite difficult to explain in layman's language," said the inventor pleasantly. "I could throw a lot of long words at you, but unless you've studied very advanced physics you really wouldn't be any the wiser. For the moment, I'd much rather give you the proof of the pudding. Would someone help me to put this on the wheelbarrow?"

The object which Simon helped him to load was shaped roughly like a large aluminium doughnut about three feet in diameter, mounted on edge on a rectangular base of the same length and some four inches thick. Also mounted on one end of the same base was an ordinary one-horse-power electric pump. A few levers, valves, dials, knobs, and nozzles protruded from the doughnut at sundry points. The entire apparatus, in spite of its massive appearance, could not have weighed much more than a hundred pounds.

At the end of the pier, they unloaded it again where several boards had been braced together with an iron plate of more recent vintage than the rest of the structure. Nemford alone jockeyed and jiggled the contraption on this footing until he could anchor it there with four enormous bolts which he had in his pockets, which fitted through holes in the base of his machine down into corresponding threaded holes in the iron floor plate, into which he tightened them with a wrench.

"This thing vibrates quite a bit," he explained, "and if it wasn't screwed down it'd shimmy right off the pier."

He lowered a thick length of hose that trailed from the pump down into the water, and plugged the pump's electrical connexion into the receptacle at the end of a conduit that ran out from the shore. The motor hummed, and after a few seconds water gushed from the output side of the pump, which at that moment was not linked with the mysterious doughnut.

"Would you test it yourself?" Nemford said to the Saint, almost apologetically. "Just so that you won't have to wonder if it really is salt."

Simon caught a spoonful in one cupped hand, and wet his lips and tongue with it. He nodded.

"It's salt."

Nemford shut off the pump and turned to Hamzah.

"Now, Colonel, those gauges you wanted to try?" The Arab produced them from a cardboard box which he had been toting mysteriously under his arm, and Nemford examined them with detached approval. "Ah, good, I see you already had them adapted for my couplings."

He helped Hamzah to install the instruments, one in the hose connexion which he completed between the pump and the doughnut, the other on what seemed to be the outlet nozzle of the system. Then he plugged the pump in again, and connected another wire from it to the main contrivance.

Once more the pump whirred; and this time the big doughnut also regurgitated, sobbed, shuddered, and settled into some quivering internal activity. Doc Nemford calmly adjusted a stopcock, and twiddled a vernier; and the output spout dribbled, spat, hiccuped, and finally began to squirt a steady stream of clear fluid which splashed over the planking and drained back down into the bay.

Nemford was complacently lighting an old battered pipe. He glanced quizzically up at the Saint over his match.

"Would you care to try a sip of that water, Mr Templar?"

Simon used his hand again to make the same test as before. The water did not exactly recall a mountain spring, as Walt Jobyn had proclaimed it, being a little too warm for that, and having some slight chemical taint which only a very sensitive palate might have detected; but it indisputably did not taste salt.

"It's fresh," he agreed, as dispassionately as he had classified the water first brought up by the pump.

"Well?" clamoured his Texan sponsor. "What more d'yuh want?"

At that moment the Saint could not have answered, even if he had been quite sure that he knew.

"I think it's a great gadget," he said cautiously.

Colonel Hamzah was not even interested in the salinity or otherwise of the water, having doubtless satisfied himself on that score in previous demonstrations. He was busily peering at his gauges, taking readings from the dials and intermittently consulting a turnip-sized stop-watch, and jotting down figures in a leather-bound notebook.

"You've noticed that the output pressure is higher than the input," Nemford said, looking over his shoulder. "That's an effect of the cyclic acceleration of the—er—well, let's call it the separating device. What you should concentrate on is the rate of flow at the output. I think you'll find it's just about as much as a pipe that size will carry—which means that you're getting fresh water as fast as you can pump."

Hamzah signified agreement with another beaming octave of dentition, and bent to examine the wire which Nemford had connected from the pump to a terminal which apparently conducted to the innards of the doughnut.

"Yes, you really should have put a meter in the circuit," Nemford clucked intuitively. "I wish you *could* take a reading on the exact amount of current it takes to operate the separator. If I tell you, you mightn't believe me. But you can see that the wire isn't any heavier than you'd find on an electric toaster, and you can feel that it isn't overheating. You don't have to be an electrical engineer for that to tell you that it isn't carrying much current. In fact, the load is only about six hundred watts. There's no hidden catch in this process, such as finding that it calls for a dollar's worth of other electric power for every penny you'd spend on pumping."

Hamzah nodded appreciatively, and made further notes in his book.

"Well, *pardner*?" Jobyn prodded, with impatient emphasis. "What d'yuh say?"

Simon took time out to light a cigarette.

It would be erroneous to assume that he regarded all inventors as crackpots or crooks. He had met all kinds; and every student of these chronicles will recall a few whose genuineness had been unquestionable from the start, and a few about whom even the Saint had guessed wrong.

"May I hear what the deal is again?" he said.

"Certainly," Nemford answered. "I'm asking two hundred thousand dollars cash for all rights. I can live very comfortably on that for the rest of my days, according to my standards, and I don't want to be bothered with royalty statements and accountants and income tax returns."

"Do you have a patent on this gizzmo?"

"I do not. If I did, the process would be available to anyone who can read, and all I'd have is the chance to spend my money on lawyers to sue anybody who infringed it. I wouldn't even have that privilege in a lot of countries that don't even recognize American patents. You don't patent guided missiles and the latest improvements in radar!"

"But what protection would we have in trying to exploit your process?"

Nemford leaned over and disconnected the pump, and shut off a valve. The motor hummed down the scale to silence, the big doughnut vibrated into stillness, and the water stopped gushing from the outlet. It became much quieter out on the pier, and easier to talk.

"If you want a patent, you can apply for one yourselves. You know that nobody's ahead of you, or the whole world would have heard of it. But a person who had a few millions to work with, like Mr Jobyn, could do a lot better, in my humble opinion. He could go to any community that desperately needs water, and build a plant at his own expense and sell water to them. He could do this all over the world. And I think he should be able to hire a few technicians who could be trusted with the secret part of the installation, which is really comparatively small. A Government, of course"—Nemford addressed himself impartially to Hamzah—"could count on men with the same security rating as they would trust with military secrets."

Simon nodded.

"But before all that, what's to stop some unscrupulous character swiping your machine somehow and opening it up to see what makes it go?"

Nemford smiled faintly.

"Naturally I've had to think of that. So I booby-trapped this model with a small charge of explosive inside. If anyone who didn't know exactly how to go about it tried to open it up, the explosion would destroy the core of the machine and probably injure him quite seriously. A similar device could protect the vital part of a full-sized plant against unauthorized prying."

Simon gazed broodingly at the remarkable engine with his hands thrust deep into his pockets. It was the kind of thing that any science-fiction writer might have fabricated, yet it was conservative in comparison with some of the marvels which humanity had become used to in the last decade. And he did not have to be convinced that there could be a fortune in it—for somebody.

He was aware that the other three were watching him expectantly, awaiting his verdict with almost embarrassing respect. Walt Jobyn was uninhibitedly fidgeting with the same eagerness that Colonel Hamzah betrayed only with the restless swivelling of his bright black eyes. Doc Nemford's attention was the most placid of the three, as if he felt completely confident that any eventual decision must be favourable to him, and even a first negative reaction would only be a temporary if tiresome setback.

Simon straightened up a little and looked at him.

"I think you've got a potential gold mine here, Doc," he said. "Or maybe I should call it something almost as good as an oil well——"

"Yiihoo!" uttered Mr Jobyn, or some similar sound. "That's my pardner. I can't wait till I hear yuh tell Felicity. But first we gotta get this deal sewed up. . . ."

He groped at his pockets, shuffling his feet in a small dance of exasperation at the minor obstructions he encountered.

Colonel Hamzah's dark bullfrog eyes had already veiled over with Pharaonic inscrutability, and he had turned away to occupy himself ostentatiously with removing the gauges that he had coupled into Nemford's miraculous plumbing.

"I'll write yuh a cheque," Jobyn said, flourishing the book that he finally found. "Ten per cent on account, just to seal the bargain. You see your lawyer fust thing tomorrow an' have him draw up somethin' that says you sold me all rights in this here doohickey. An' tell him to make it short an' straight so even I can understand it. If I have to get another lawyer to translate it, I don't want it."

"I don't need your deposit," Nemford said awkwardly.

"I'll take your word that you mean business. And I can put down a sale of all rights myself in a few lines. I sympathize with your point of view about that—if it's a straightforward deal, there's no need for twenty pages of hedging. But. . . ."

"But what, man?"

Nemford's embarrassment had become so acute that he seemed to wish he had starved before he ever offered his discovery for sale.

"Well . . . when we wind this up, I'll turn over this model to you, without the booby trap, and all my specifications and blueprints. Now, if you changed your mind an hour later, and decided to stop payment on your cheque for the full price, you'd still have everything of mine, and you could have had my drawings copied a hundred times, and all I could do would be to sue you . . . Of course I'm not suggesting that you *would*; but you *could*. After all, I don't really know anything about you, except that you're *supposed* to own a lot of oil wells. Do you understand?"

Walt Jobyn stared at him for a moment, with his weathered face taking on a slight tinge of beetroot; and then he let out an equine squeal of laughter and slapped the inventor resoundingly on the back.

"Well, fan mah britches," he chortled. "You're as right as yuh can be, Doc, an' yuh had the guts to come straight out with it. I like that. Okay, then, you tell me how yuh think we should do it."

"I'd be scared to death to have all that money in cash," Nemford said. "But cashier's cheques are just about as final, aren't they? I mean, you can't stop them or take them back. You could give me five of them, say, for forty thousand each, so that I could put them in different banks as I'd probably want to. But as soon as you gave them to me, I'd hand everything over."

"If that'll make yuh happy, Doc, that's the way it'll be." Jobyn frowned. "But it'll be the day after tomorrow at the soonest before I can get those cheques from my bank in Texas, unless I charter a private plane to fetch 'em."

"That's all right, Mr Jobyn," Nemford said, with his normal composure coming back again. "Whenever they get here, you can give me a call and come over and we'll make the exchange."

"Provided somebody hasn't stolen those blueprints meanwhile," Simon put in. "Or are they booby-trapped, too?"

Nemford shook his head.

"I don't think they need to be. They're in a safe deposit box at my bank."

"I won't even ask yuh which bank, Doc," Jobyn said jovially, "in case yuh think I might put Mr Templar here up to bustin' into it."

The joke did not seem to make any special impression on his audience.

"That's fine, then," Nemford said with an air of sober relief, and picked up his wrench to attack the bolts that secured his model. "Now if you won't mind helping me get this back to the house. . . ."

They assisted him to load his machine back on the wheelbarrow and cart it back to the shore, and there Jobyn held out his hand.

"We made a deal, Doc," he said heartily. "I'll be talkin' to yuh soon with them cheques in mah hand. An' when yuh feel like takin' a trip somewhere, you should come to Texas an' *see* mah oil wells."

He offered the same hand to Hamzah.

"Too bad yuh lost out, Colonel," he said generously. "You should've made up your mind quicker—yuh could easily, not havin' to listen to a back-seat-drivin' wife, like me. Even if yuh got a dozen of 'em, you fellas got enough sense to keep 'em locked up in a harem. But better luck next time, anyhow."

The Arabian delegate accepted the hand gingerly, and winced at the shake, but managed a toothily courteous grimace.

"Y'know, pardner," Jobyn observed as they drove away, "Felicity's goin' to be spittin' like a scalded bobcat when she hears this water-makin' invention is as genuine as I been tellin' her all along. She'll like to tear your hair out for backin' me up."

"I can imagine that," said the Saint. "So since she isn't my wife, I'd just as soon pass up that exhilarating privilege, if it's all the same to you."

Jobyn seemed to wilt slightly in the mid-act of igniting a celebratory cigar of sufficient calibre to have defended the Alamo.

"But I was countin' on *you* to——"

"Why should either of us ask for trouble? Is there any law in Texas that everything has to be done in your joint names? Does she add up your bank statement every month? Does it take both your signatures to write a cheque?"

"No, but——"

"I'll bet that when you were courting, Walt, you thought she'd be a right cute little filly to rope and tie. But not so long after she had your name on a marriage licence, you found she'd grown into a bucking bronco—and she was riding you!"

"How did yuh know that?"

"One day I'm going to write a book about the Great American Wife. But meanwhile I'll give you a free preview of the last chapter. It says : she's only the fault of the Great American Husband. He gave up too easily. I suppose it's too late for him to go back to the good healthy custom of belting her in the mouth any time she opens it out of turn. But if she wants to make out she's so much smarter than he is, on strictly intellectual terms, then he's got a right to outsmart her if he can."

Mr Jobyn squinted up at him sidelong.

"What yuh gettin' at, Mr Templar?"

"You said it yourself to Hamzah. However many wives he's got, he keeps 'em locked up and he doesn't tell them about his business. Now, you could hardly start a harem with Felicity, but she's only one, and you should be able to handle her. Go back and tell her you still think Nemford has a gold mine, and I said it looked good, too, but in deference to her great wisdom you decided not to invest in it. This makes her love you to death; but inside, she wonders. . . ."

"But——"

"Then you go right ahead with what you already decided. And after it's made you a few millions, the next time she's getting really ornery, you can say: 'Now I come to think of it, sweetheart, I forgot to tell you how much I made out of the last time I didn't take your advice.' And you sock her with the figures, for the first time . . . On the other hand, until this deal does pay off, and even if by sheer bad luck it never does, you'll never have to squirm while she tells you what a dope you were."

The immediate representative of the second biggest of the United States mulled this shamelessly pragmatic proposition under an intensely corrugated brow for several seconds, and came up jubilantly slapping his thigh.

"Goll dang it," he said exuberantly, "I think yuh got the answer I was lookin' for. An' I ain't the man to forget it. How much do *you* figure to invest in this here process?"

"Not much more than I already have," said the Saint. "With taxes the way they are, I can't afford to be a millionaire; and I can't take a profit from giving matrimonial advice without losing my amateur standing. But some day if I get desperate I may stop at one of your wells with a bucket."

He dropped Jobyn at the hotel in La Jolla, and firmly declined to stay for dinner or even for a drink, claiming that he was already overdue at the home of the friends he had been on his way to visit in San Diego.

"If you're going to play it the way I suggested, you shouldn't need any moral support when you talk to Felicity. Not at this stage, anyway," he said. "But I'll give you the phone number where I'm staying, and you can call me any time you have qualms."

For his host he had a slightly different story, merely to avert the tedium of more complicated explanations.

"I have to see a fellow at Mission Beach about a small business deal that a pal of mine asked me to check on," he said with careful casualness, as they were finishing dinner. "D'you mind if I run over there and join you at the Yacht Club later? It shouldn't take me an hour, at the very worst."

He had memorized the location of Doc Nemford's shack so accurately that he did not need to drive within a hundred yards of it. He parked his car an inconspicuous block away, and strolled down an alley with a chipped and faded signboard at the entrance that offered *Boats & Bait*.

Simon had seen the boats from Nemford's jetty, and had been less than excited as a nautical connoisseur. At close quarters they looked even less picturesque and more unseaworthy; but he was not planning an extended cruise. There were no oars or other conventional means of propulsion in sight, the livery operator having no doubt thoughtfully secured them inside the padlocked shed from which he did his business, but the Saint did not have to search far for a discarded four-foot piece of board that would serve as an adequate paddle for the voyage he had in mind.

He quietly nursed the least leaky skiff he could select along the shore line to Nemford's property, and let it drift up to the pier and even under it.

There was only a half moon that night, and the sky was murky, but Simon had a pencil flashlight to help him in the dark corners, though he used it with the most furtive discretion. He verified certain structural possibilities that had intrigued him, and then hitched the painter to one of the pilings and swung himself nimbly up on to the decking.

There was a glow of light behind the ground-floor curtains of Nemford's cottage, and the Saint moved like a drifting shadow towards an open window until the murmur of voices inside resolved itself into distinct words and equally clear identifications of the speakers.

The first to emerge into this unconscious clarity was Nemford himself, who was saying : "You're asking me to go back on my word to Mr Jobyn. I know we haven't signed anything yet, but we shook hands on a deal."

Simon could not see into the room from any angle, but the accent and context of the next speech made visual confirmation supererogatory.

"I appreciate your problem, Doctor, and I am prepared to compensate you for your embarrassment. I have spoken by telephone to Cairo, and I am authorized to pay you fifty thousand dollars more to change your mind about this bargain with Mr Jobyn. I am sure that if he changed his mind, *he* would not be bound by the handshake."

"But suppose, then, he wanted to offer me more?"

"If you accept my price, you need not be here to listen to him. Perhaps it would be wiser if you were not, in case he is only angry. But I cannot haggle as in a bazaar. I was talking to you first, I remind you, and I deserved the right to make the first bid. But since I make the second, it is also the last for me. A quarter of a million dollars, Doctor. The extra money will almost pay your tax on the transaction."

There was a pause.

"But when would you expect to pay me, Colonel? You remember, I had to tell Mr Jobyn that I only had his word for his oil wells. I hate to say this sort of thing, but after all, how do I know that your Government will back you up? And meanwhile, if I alienate Mr Jobyn——"

"My Embassy is being ordered tonight to let me have the money. As soon as the bank is open in Washington tomorrow morning, they can send it to me. Because of the time difference, it can arrive here as soon as the banks open in San Diego. Tell me which bank you keep your papers in, and I'll have it sent there. We meet, I give you the money, you give me the blueprints. It is so simple."

"What about the model?"

"Aha. We take it with us to the bank, in a taxi. The taxi waits. When we have finished, I take the taxi to the airport. My Government would not pay so much money to compete with Mr Jobyn, it means very much to our prestige to have your invention exclusively. Of course you would not think of giving him the model with some more blueprints—you are an honourable man—but I am ordered to bring it with me, and my suggestion is most practical."

The craftily candid exposure of teeth that must have accompanied this could be heard in the voice.

"Would you be leaving at once?"

"Yes, you will have to face Mr Jobyn alone. If you decide to wait for him. But I am afraid your Government might take his part if they knew I was taking away something they might officially lend to us for political considerations. I expect to be highly commended if I make that impossible. So, I would prefer to be out of your country before anyone complains."

Another pause.

Simon could picture Doc Nemford chewing on his pipe, his tall, taut brow furrowed with earnest deliberation.

At last——

"All right, Colonel. I'll have to accept. I just want you to realize that I'm not being influenced by the price you're offering. The reason is, I'm ashamed of having almost let you down. As you had to remind, you *were* the first customer. But with Mr Jobyn throwing his oil wells at me, and that chap he brought with him today——"

"Who was he?"

"One of the world's greatest experts in this field, though you'd never guess it to look at him. But when *he* said my invention looked good, I knew I'd never be able to stop Mr Jobyn elbowing you out of the way."

"Do not feel too unhappy about him," Hamzah said magnanimously. "He still can throw his oil wells somewhere else. Now, let us set a time. I will call for you at ten o'clock. By then, I shall have made a box in which your model can be packed, and you will have removed the explosive. With your permission, I will take the measurements. . . ."

Simon had no need to hear any more. He retreated as softly as he had approached, lowered himself into the dinghy, and paddled it silently back to where he had borrowed it.

He was at the Yacht Club within the hour he had allotted for the detour, and wholeheartedly enjoyed the rest of an unimportant evening without thinking it necessary to say any more about his brief digression. Nor did he feel obliged to spoil Walt Jobyn's evening by phoning him that night.

Even after a large late breakfast the next morning he was not overpowered by any urge to make the call, but took a much livelier interest in the fact that it looked like a perfect day to go sailing, as had been tentatively proposed before they went to bed.

"I'm afraid I'll hold you up a bit, though," he said. "I've got to drop by and see this merchant I visited last night again. Some papers I have to see were at his bank, and he's getting them out this morning. I can't put it off, because one of the characters involved is catching a plane east around midday. Could we meet at the Club for an early lunch and blast off right afterwards?"

It may be interesting for some future analyst to note that for a man of such complicated activities the Saint seldom found himself constrained to lie. He could nearly always phrase the literal truth in such a way that the listener received the exact impression that the Saint wanted him to have. It was a technique which eliminated all the hazardous overhead of keeping conflicting stories straight and mutually harmonious, while at the same time adding a certain private spice to what might otherwise have been mere routine dialogue.

In this case, it also won the Saint a sufficient margin of unquestioned time, during which he could drive peacefully back to Mission Beach, with no unseemly desperate eye glued to the clock and mileometer, and arrive within sight of the front entrance of Doc Nemford's shack, near the same parking spot that he had found before, at a moment intelligently calculated to succeed the Nemford-Hamzah safari to the bank, but also to precede the predictable return of Nemford alone.

Thus when Doc Nemford walked back into his own temporary home, a little before noon, he found a lean bronze-faced man comfortably extended between the best chair in the living-room and the handiest table-top on which a pair of very long legs could conveniently park their extremities.

"Come on in, Doc," Simon encouraged him hospitably. "I hope you don't mind me making myself at home."

"No, why not?" Nemford said with pardonable vagueness. "If I'd known you were coming—but I wasn't expecting Mr Jobyn till tomorrow——"

"Let's both save a little time," Simon suggested soothingly. "I'll put my cards on the table, and you do the same, and we'll work out the score like well-brought-up scientists. I was still trying to make up my mind whether you knew who I was, right up until I heard you give Hamzah the clincher last night. Well, as one of the world's greatest experts in this field, though you'd never guess it to look at me, I'd like to give you an award as the best player of a busted flush that I've sat in with in a long elegy of these games. Once the chips began to fly, you squeezed your hand to the last pip."

Doc Nemford fumbled out his pipe and pouch and began the restorative mechanisms of stoking one from the other.

"What else could I do?" he said. "You kept me guessing yourself—right up until now, I was trying to decide whether I'd fooled you."

"You weren't so far from it, chum. You had a nice explanation of why the fresh water came out of your gadget with more pressure than you were pumping the sea water in—but if you ever do it again, it'd be better to put a pressure reducer in the circuit and not have to explain anything. Sometimes these city water systems carry an awful head of steam. . . . You don't have anything like that to worry about with the electric consumption, even if someone like Hamzah did hook a meter into the line : I'm sure the vibrator inside your model doesn't draw a lot of extra juice. . . . And even the valve that you open and shut when you're demonstrating doesn't give away the gimmick—in fact, it's a good piece of business."

"Then what actually did make you suspicious?"

"First off, only my own low dishonest mind. If I'd stood and watched the Red Sea open for the Israelites, the first thing I'd've wondered about was how it might have been faked. Now, the way that pier of yours is built is probably a perfectly common method of construction, but to me it suggested plumbing. And that gave me the idea that in a tubular tangle of that kind, nobody else might notice a couple of extra pipes—one of 'em joined into a piling to take the pumped-up bay water back where it came from, and the other running back to shore to connect with your house supply. Then I tried to figure out how a crook could switch the flow——"

"And how could he?"

"With a base plate set in the dock, to which he would bolt the base of his ingenious gizzmo, using outsize bolts that he took from his pocket and put back there, and which were the only incidental equipment that nobody got a good look at. Bolts which I'm certain are hollow, with outlets in the right places, so that when you screw them down they become the most miraculous part of your invention. One of 'em side-tracks the salt water you're pumping up, and the other takes in the fresh water which is one of the civic amenities for which you are privileged to pay taxes on this dump."

"And on this imaginative basis alone——"

"No, I'm not supernatural. I didn't have any more to start with than an interesting doubt. But before I carried it to the bitter end—which included a rather minute study of the pipe connexions underneath your pier last night—I'd convinced myself with a rather more arbitrary test."

"And what was that?" Nemford inquired, with the intensest unfeigned interest.

"I'd tasted your manufactured fresh water," said the Saint. "I happen to have rather sensitive taste buds, which I have raised on a diet of the best vintage wines. They aren't so familiar with water, unless it was splashing down a mountain trout stream. But they can still recognize the tang of chlorine in a city supply."

Nemford sucked at his pipe, holding a match steadily over the bowl.

"You deserve all the things I've heard about you," he said. "But why didn't you say any of this yesterday?"

"I was interested to see how the scenario would work out. If you won't think I'm being patronizing, I'd call it a kind of nostalgia. I admired a lot of touches in your technique. You handled the financial angles brilliantly—just the right pressure where it would do the most good. And I know you'll do well with those traveller's cheques you were talking about—you can cash them abroad in so many places where they don't ask questions."

Doc Nemford made a deprecating gesture.

"I'm trying to make a living, like the rest of us, Saint."

"And I'm not greedy. I told Jobyn I thought you had a good deal, because I figured that would bring Hamzah back with a higher bid, and so I'd be keeping Jobyn out of trouble. But at the same time it was a help to you, and my dear old grandmother taught me never to take part in a swindle unless I made something out of it for myself."

Doc Nemford nodded philosophically.

"How much do you want?"

"I'll settle for fifty thousand dollars, which I earned for you anyhow, so you shouldn't begrudge it. And you can write Jobyn a letter and tell him you're sorry to renege on the deal but you couldn't resist that extra dough—and see that you've left town before he receives it."

Nemford took from his wallet a small sheaf of cashier's cheques, selected one, and endorsed it on the back to the order of Simon Templar.

"You're a lot fairer than I thought you'd be," he said. "In fact, I didn't think you'd let me get away with anything if you were wise to me."

"Frankly, if the victim had been almost anyone else, I wouldn't, Doc. But now for the rest of my life I can dream of the expression on Nasser's face, when Hamzah arrives with his trophies and they find out what they've bought. I shall feel that I've personally done something about Foreign Aid," said the Saint.

The Gentle Ladies

"ALL I can say," Kathleen Holland said inadequately, "is that he's a *creep*."

"The world is crawling with them," smiled the Saint sympathetically. "But unfortunately it isn't a statutory offence yet. And if I tried to exterminate them all myself, just on general principles, I wouldn't have any time left to steal a living. There has to be something specific about his creepiness."

"But I thought that's what you'd be able to find out!"

Simon Templar looked at her again. She had a face with bone in it : definite cheekbones and a strong jaw, a nose short but sculptured. She wore her thick chestnut hair almost without a wave, in a kind of abbreviated page-boy bob—obviously not because it was fashionable at the time, which it wasn't, but because it suited her. Her hazel eyes were very lively and her chiselled lips framed a wide and potentially careless mouth.

"You'd have to tell me a lot more about him," he said. "Perhaps if you weren't so tied up with this charitable den of iniquity——"

"I can soon fix that," she said. "There are more gals trying to help around here than you could shake a swizzle stick at. I'll just tell the Mother Superior that I'm taking time out, and I'll be all yours."

She left him in the crêpe-paper arbour where he had had her alone for a few minutes, and headed quickly and decisively for the gingham-clothed central table where a bevy of other eager maidens were cajoling the wandering citizenry to buy dollops of what the hand-lettered signs proclaimed to be champagne punch, ladled from a cut-glass bowl the size of a bathtub in which had been stirred, together with several gallons of miscellaneous sodas and fruit juices (the Saint's sensitive palate assured him), at least a magnum of genuine Bollinger.

Of all the unlikely surroundings in which the Saint might be discovered, a church bazaar, despite his canonical nickname, is certainly as implausible as any; but by this time he was getting so used to finding himself in improbable places that he had developed a form of philosophical passivity which might as well be emulated, if only in self-defence, by anyone who intends to follow him through many of these episodes.

The town of Santa Barbara, little more than two hours of freeway driving up the coast from Los Angeles, is California's most jealous curator of its Spanish heritage. While the great sprawling monster that was once leisurely known as *El Pueblo de Nuestra Señora la Reina de los Angeles* has lopped off all but the last two words of its historic name and surrendered itself to modern industry and smog, Santa Barbara seems to have decided that the twentieth century is the transient guest, and to be trying like a good house-keeper to keep things as much as possible the way the Conquistadors would like to find it when they come back. In the whole city not a tenth of the streets have North American names, the most conspicuous of them being State Street, which appropriately enough is the main stem of shops and offices and suchlike parvenu incursions. But flanking it are Chapala and Anacapa, and the street crossing it ring with such names as Cabrillo, Figueroa, Ortega, and Gutierrez. And yet with all this Hispanic tradition there is also a social cult which leans towards institutions more commonly associated with squirearchy of Old England, such as horse shows, flower shows, garden parties, fund-raising teas, and parochial fêtes like the one which had ensnared such an unprecedented patron as Simon Templar.

The better-looking half of the couple of old friends he was visiting had said firmly : "I've been roped into running the popgun shooting gallery all day long at this brawl, and the least you can do is drop by and relieve me for half an hour." But when he dutifully showed up, she had inspected him again and said : "There's a wicked gleam in your eye that makes me suspect that you'd be telling the kids to turn the popguns on the behinds of some of the passing dowagers. I'll let you buy me a champagne punch instead, and introduce you to a pretty girl who'll keep your mind on more grown-up ways of getting into trouble."

Thus he had met Kathleen Holland; and, after his hostess had excused herself to hurry back to her stall, what might have been a more idly flirtatious encounter had become a half-serious discussion of the creepiness of Mr Alton Powls.

The Saint was almost automatically prejudiced against Mr Powls, but he could be impersonal enough to realize that Mr Powls might never even have squeezed his name into the conversation but for the reaction that the Saint's own name evoked from most people who heard it. Kathleen Holland was a real estate agent and by all ordinary criteria a down-to-earth young business woman; but she was no less ordinary in assuming that the Saint was ready to take off like a bloodhound on any scent that was offered him. However, in her case the presumption was not so hard to take.

"You see," she said, when she returned without the apron that was her badge of office, and was thereby transformed into another customer like himself, and they were strolling anonymously through the crowd in search of a more secluded place to continue the session, "I feel I'm partly responsible. I should have known there was something wrong when he asked so many questions about Aunt Flo."

"The world seems to be infested with Aunts, too," Simon observed philosophically. "But it isn't necessarily a felony to ask questions about them. What has this one done?"

"Nothing, of course. I know you don't live here, but when you meet her you'll know how ridiculous that sounds. But you can say anything you think, because she isn't really *my* aunt."

Miss Florence Warshed, it appeared, was known to everyone within her social stratum in Santa Barbara as "Aunt Flo," because that was the way she was known to the two nieces who lived with her, and that was the way she liked it, and whatever Aunt Flo liked had a way of becoming the way things were done, at least in her nearest vicinity.

Miss Warshed had settled herself immovably upon the Santa Barbara landscape about twenty years ago, escorted by the two nieces from whom she derived her popular title, with the purchase of a large rambling house in the older but most respectable section of town, where they set up a ménage which in some other localities might have been deemed at least eccentric but which in the cloistered atmosphere of that corner of that city was only considered quaint and nostalgically delightful. For the two junior Misses Warshed, it was soon revealed to those who pursued the inquiry, were the daughters of a vaguely disreputable elder brother of Aunt Flo who abandoned them to the care of a wife who soon afterwards died of mortification or some such obsolete ailment, thus leaving their maiden aunt Flo to rear them, which she had done more devotedly than any natural mother. If Aunt Flo had ever had any procreative urges of her own, they seemed to have been completely sublimated by the responsibilities of this foster brood; and if some local amateur psychologists surmised that she had subtly instilled her own spinsterish diathesis into her charges, it could have been just as validly argued that they had grown up with androphobic prejudices of their very own, germinating from the embarrassment of having a father whom they could not even identify in a picture and whose name they had never heard mentioned except with the most icily significant restraint. At any rate, their lives had never been overtly complicated by romance, let alone marriage: Aunt Flo had been safely past her half-century when she hit the town, and both her protégées had been well into their late thirties, so that there had been no immediate problem of fending off slavering suitors. And seemingly content to age gracefully as they had arrived, they had remained an inviolable trio while Aunt Flo decayed gradually into her more obstreperous seventies and the waifs she had sponsored faded gracefully into their late but unlamented fifties, all of them being wistfully but intolerably charming all the time. To keep themselves healthily occupied and also pay the rent, they had opened a shop in the bypassed suburb of Montecito, inevitably named *Ye Needle Nooke*, where the products of their knitting and crochet implements were on sale at outrageous prices and were regularly bought by transient tourists and an indispensable core of locals who thought that the Warshed Sisters were just *too* sweet and should be subsidized on principle.

"And they are sweet, too," Kathleen said. "It just breaks your heart sometimes to think how much they could've given some man and never had a chance to. All right, so I should go back to the bottom of the grammar class. But you've got to meet them yourself. Come on over here."

Before he could mount an effective delaying action she was practically dragging him through the crowd again on another tangent that led to a concession which could be instantly identified as one of the prime attractions of the affair. All it was actually selling was cheaply printed cards ruled into squares in each of which appeared some random number; but the sign over the entrance said BINGO, and this magic word seemed to have been sufficient to enchant an extraordinary number of devout numerologists into purchasing one or more of these mystic plaques.

"Just one thing—don't give my real name," was about all the Saint had time and presence of mind enough to throw into her ear, before they were being welcomed into the fold by a delightfully frail and faded blonde in pastel-flowered chiffon who said: "Why, Kathleen, honey, are you going to try your luck with us? That's what I call doing double your duty."

"This is Violet Warshed," Kathleen said, and completed the introduction with: "This is Mr—er—Templeton. He's been such a good customer for the champagne punch that I thought I ought to share him a bit."

"Why, that's what I call giving till it must hurt, honey," Violet Warshed put out a soft hand that would have been only perfunctory if it had not had a slight tendency to cling. "I hope this is your lucky day, Mr Templeton, truly I do."

She must have been quite a doll thirty-five years ago, Simon thought without disparagement. A Marilyn Monroe type in her generation, probably, wide open to caricature, but overflowing with everything that it took to evoke the protective instincts of the male. It was almost incredible that that appeal should have failed to inglutinate a husband when it was at its lushest, but it was still working in an entirely wistful way which Simon could see would confirm the local assumption that the Warshed waifs had to be Taken Care Of.

He sat down with Kathleen at the end of one of the long tables which were occupied to the verge of capacity by a horde of philanthropists brooding over their charts of destiny and marking off occasional rectangles on them as the fateful numbers boomed out through a badly adjusted complex of loudspeakers. An iron-grey woman in the same indefinite fifties as Violet Warshed bustled up and down the aisles between the tables, repeating the numbers that were called and helping the more dim-sighted devotees of this intoxicating sport to mark the right squares on their cards. As she got down to the end of the next table she recognized Kathleen and said : "Oh, a trespasser." Then she saw the Saint and linked them together, and said : "Well, it's about time you had a good man, Kathy. Where did you find him ?"

"This is Ida Warshed," Kathleen said. With the facility of practice, she went on : "And this is Mr Templeton. He's been such a good customer that I thought——"

"Don't ever stop to think, dearie. If he looks like a good customer, he's in. What was that name again ?"

Even at her age Ida Warshed had a twinkle in her eye, and one got an impression that in her extreme youth she might have been quite a handful. She was as buxom and earthy as Violet was ethereal. In fact, if they had not been introduced as sisters no one would have been likely to guess that they were even remotely related. The only theory Simon could hazard was that by some freak of genetics each of them had inherited the characteristics of one parent to the almost complete exclusion of the other —Ida perhaps being predominantly the image of the scapegrace father, while Violet might have mirrored the abandoned mother who had pined away.

"Now do you have an idea what they're like?" Kathleen asked, as Ida went on her busy way.

"Well, vaguely," said the Saint, mechanically circling a number on his card with one of the coloured crayons provided for the purpose. "But——"

"That's Aunt Flo," she said, "up there on the platform."

At the focal point of the long tables where the congregation sat there was a high dais draped in bunting, not much larger than was necessary to accommodate a small table and a straight-backed chair. In the chair sat a large angular woman whose back was just as straight, even if braced by obvious tight-drawn corsets. Over the corsets she wore a black satin dress that made no attempt to be modern in length or cut, with a high boned collar of white lace and matching frills of lace at the wrists. To offset this austerity, however, her fingernails were lacquered pearl-grey, her lipstick was dark red, and her white hair had been rinsed with blue. Her face must once have been handsome rather than pretty, but age had not hardened it; indeed, the wrinkles it had acquired seemed to have engraved it with an indelible pattern of kindliness and serenity.

She twirled a wire cage filled with numbered balls, and when it came to rest she manipulated a sort of valve at the bottom which laid a single ball on the table like an egg; she read the number without glasses, and called it into her microphone in a strong firm voice. Simon drew another circle on his card.

"For a dame of her age, she seems to be in rare shape," he remarked.

"You don't know the half of it," Kathleen said. "She must be at least seventy-five, but she drives the car to market and does all the shopping and most of the cooking at home. And don't let that Whistler's-Mother look fool you—she's never stopped being the head of the family. Violet and Ida still do what she tells them, just as if they were nearer sixteen than sixty. It's almost funny to hear them ask her if they may go to a movie, if she doesn't want to see it herself, and she tells them what time they have to be home."

"But," said the Saint, "I still don't see what all this has to do with the creep you started with, Brother Powls."

"Because ever since he came here they've been under some awful strain, as if—well, it's silly, but I can only say as if he was *haunting* them. I don't believe in that kind of hypnotism, but if it isn't that, he must have some other hold over them, and now that you've met them you can see that that sounds almost as ridiculous."

Mr Alton Powls had come upon the scene by simply walking into the office where Kathleen Holland worked. The office opened on a pseudo-Andalusian inside patio which it shared with about a dozen shops mostly dedicated to the sale of antiques, jewellery, *objets d'art*, paintings, books, and similar preciosa, all enterprises ideally suited to a location close to but architecturally shut off from the commercial hurly-burly of State Street, where shoppers could browse at leisure in an atmosphere of olde-worlde tranquillity which did much to blunt their apperception of the fact that they were being charged strictly new-world prices. Directly across the patio were the premises of *Ye Needle Nooke*; and through its large plate-glass window, from Kathleen's window, could be plainly seen the Warshed sisters at work, Violet sewing and Ida rearranging the displays of merchandise, while Aunt Flo busied herself with correspondence or bookkeeping at a desk in the background.

"Do you happen to know those ladies across the way?" he asked.

She had not yet identified him as a Creep, but only as

an elderly gentleman not especially different from any of the other idle strollers in the courtyard, and so she agreeably told him the names. The first evidence of Creepiness he gave was in his reaction to them : she was sure that they brought a gleam of recognition which was instantly veiled.

"Would they be from Milwaukee?" he queried.

"No, they came from Kansas City."

"Was that long ago?"

"It was soon after I was born, anyway."

He looked at her calculatingly.

"They remind me of some people I knew a long time ago," he said. "I think I'll go and talk to them."

He went out and across the patio, and she could not help watching the rest from her desk. It was as graphic and at the same time as baffling as a movie on which the sound track had gone dead.

He went into *Ye Needle Nooke*, and Ida Warshed met him with the mechanical cordiality with which she would have greeted any stranger who walked in. She could only have asked, quite impersonally, what she could do for him. But his answer seemed to stop her cold. She stood there, transfixed, all the life fading out of her face. For the longest time, she seemed bereft of any power of movement, as well as speech. Then, in a most uncharacteristically feeble and helpless way, she make a beckoning gesture at Violet.

Violet put down her sewing and came over, wearing the same perfunctory smile in her more fragile and wispier way. Mr Powls spoke again. Violet froze as Ida had done, and then looked at Ida helplessly. Then both of them, by simultaneous consent, looked appealingly at Aunt Flo.

Aunt Flo put down her pen and came over from her desk. But on her candid competent face there was no more immediate response than had been shown by either of her nieces. Until Mr Powls repeated something that he had obviously said before.

Aunt Flo also froze, momentarily. But there was no one beyond her to appeal. And so after that moment she began to talk, quite volubly, in a tone that the frequent shakings of her head made vehemently negative. But Mr Powls seemed only to persist with whatever he was maintaining. There was another Creepy quality, Kathleen thought, in the implacable way he stood his ground, answering mostly with shrugs that somehow had an offensive insincerity.

Presently he turned and left the shop and sauntered away. But after his departure there was none of the complacency of three embattled women who had triumphantly repulsed an obnoxious male. There was the inevitable first minute when they all talked at once, but it quickly subsided into a bleak despondency in which they all seemed at a total loss for anything to say. Ida kicked moodily at a chair-leg, Violet dabbed the corners of her eyes with a handkerchief, and Aunt Flo sat down at her desk again, heavily, and rested her forehead on her clenched hands.

Then Violet happened to glance straight across the patio at Kathleen, and said something to Ida, who glanced in the same direction; and Kathleen suddenly felt like an eavesdropper and buried herself in the papers she had been working on before the interruption.

Later that afternoon, as the shops on the patio were preparing to close up, Aunt Flo came over on the pretext of asking if Kathleen could recommend a part-time gardener to take over some of the heavy work on the flower beds which were the Warsheds' principal hobby and exercise as well as their most harmless pride. After that gambit had served its purpose, she said with transparent casualness : "What did you think of that man who came looking for us a little while ago?"

"I didn't know he was looking for you," Kathleen said. "He told me he thought he knew you from somewhere away back."

She recited her conversation with Mr Powls almost verbatim, but without any commentary.

"Is that all he said?"

"Yes—as far as I can remember."

Aunt Flo's birdlike eyes raked through her like affectionate needles.

"I think he's a crank," she said. "He tried to insist that he knew us, but none of us ever saw him before. We couldn't all three be mistaken. You'd better watch out if you see him again. It's those kind of people who are never suspected until they turn out to be Monsters."

Although the word Monster was no more than an earlier synonym for Creep, it was not that echo of her own thinking that brushed Kathleen with a clammy chill. It was the incontrovertible certainty, after what she had recently witnessed, that Aunt Flo was lying.

Four days passed before she saw Mr Powls again. She happened to look up, and he was back in *Ye Needle Nooke*, talking to the three ladies. He seemed to have been showing them something like a fairly large newspaper clipping, which he took back and folded carefully and put away in his wallet. Only a few more words were spoken after that, before he turned and came out; she could see very little of how they acted after his exit, for he blocked the view almost completely by walking straight across the patio to her office.

She tried not to appear too hurried over her conventional "Good afternoon" but couldn't help going on, disingenuous though it had to sound, with: "I hear you didn't know the Warsheds after all."

"Oh, but I do," he said. "And they remember me now. I've been able to convince them."

She flicked a glance through the window, but could only see that the ladies were in some kind of huddle at the back of the shop.

"I've been back to Kansas City since I saw you last," he said. "But I've decided that Santa Barbara has it beat. I think I'll settle down here. Could you show me a very small furnished cottage or a nice little apartment?"

She took him to a couple of places she had listed, and he was delighted with the second, a sub-let that had been put in her hands only the previous day. Then came the routine question of references.

"The Misses Warshed should be good enough for any-one here, shouldn't they?" he said blandly, and she would have sworn that he struggled to hide his malicious enjoyment of a private joke.

However, she now had an unimpeachable reason for re-opening the subject with Aunt Flo.

"We were mistaken," Aunt Flo said with tight lips. "It's terribly easy to forget things after twenty years, especially when you get to be my age. But of course we knew Mr Powls back in Kansas City. I hope you'll be able to put out of your mind the things I said about him the other day, because it's most embarrassing to me to think that I could have been so wrong."

She was very gallant, very much the *grande dame*. Beside her, the sisters nodded in docile corroboration.

"Then I can take it that he's all right—I mean, he'll be good for the rent, and all that sort of thing?"

"Yes, dear, he will be."

"What kind of business was he in, in Kansas City?"

Violet and Ida looked at each other, and then mutely at Aunt Flo, leaving her to answer.

"He was a general business man," Aunt Flo said firmly. "He was mixed up in lots of big deals. I don't profess to understand these things that men get involved in. But he was very successful."

"He was a big spender, too," Ida put in.

Violet nodded. And that was all they had to say. Which in itself was strange enough, for normally they loved to gossip about people—of course in the nicest way.

Mr Powls himself was no more communicative when Kathleen tried to question him.

"I've been in and out of so many things," he said, with a carefully impressive air of modesty in his vagueness. "Buying and selling—importing and exporting—stocks and bonds. But I'm retired now. So it would bore me as much to tell you my life story as you'd be bored listening to it. And it doesn't really matter, does it? You only want to be sure that I won't have wild parties or move out with the landlord's furniture, and I know the Misses Warshed have vouched for that."

She did not know how to press the question further without seeming gratuitously impertinent.

"So," she told the Saint, "he's been here ever since. He pays his rent on the dot, and he takes good care of the place. He asked me to get him a cleaning woman to come in once a week, so I was able to check on that through her. Sometimes I see him around town, and he's always perfectly at ease and polite. Perhaps he *is* just a retired business man leading a quiet bachelor life, but——"

Simon drew another circle on his card.

"Presumably he pays the rent by cheque—you wouldn't have thought of making any inquiries at his bank?"

She actually giggled.

"*Touché*. That's how horribly inquisitive I can be when I start. I told them I'd been asked to get a bank reference on him, but between what they didn't know and what they weren't allowed to say I didn't get very much.

But his account is quite small, and he mostly deposits cash."

The Saint's brows suddenly drew together.

"Cash? You have an item there."

"That's what I thought. He isn't working in any job, that I know of."

"Does he see much of the Warsheds, since they've decided they know him?"

"I've seen him at their house twice," Kathleen said. "They invite me sometimes, when they have a little party. You wouldn't think they'd want an extra girl, but they're very considerate about things like that, and if for any reason they've got a man coming who's younger than any of them, they beg me to come and prove that they aren't ganging up on him themselves. Well, each time, it was obvious that the idea was to help Mr Powls meet some local people. And yet I just *knew* that they weren't a bit happy about it. Not that they didn't try to do it well. In fact, they were trying too hard—they were much too busy and eager and chattery, even for them. As if they were under a frightful strain and trying to cover up. And yet he wasn't pointing a gun at them, like the gangsters did at the family in that movie."

"There are metaphorical guns, too," Simon said. "How did the Creep behave?"

"Just like anybody else. Only he kept making *me* think of a cat watching a cage of birds. I suppose by this time you're convinced that I'm thoroughly neurotic and——"

The Saint said, abruptly: "Bingo!"

He stood up, waving his card.

"Would you bring your card up here, please," said Aunt Flo.

Kathleen recovered from her momentary blankness and went to the dais with him to introduce him.

"A friend of yours? How nice, dear," said Aunt Flo,

nevertheless checking the numbers which the Saint had ringed with the emotionless efficiency of a seasoned cashier. "Yes, this is right." She said into her microphone: "We have a winner, girls. Pick up the old cards, and we'll start a new game." She counted out fifty dollars from a partitioned tray in front of her, and gave them to the Saint, and said: "Congratulations, Mr Templeton. Are you having a good time?"

"So good that it doesn't seem right to make a profit out of it." Simon shuffled the prize money, put half of it in his pocket, re-folded the rest, and held it out to the old lady. "May I put this back in the fund, as a donation?"

"You're very generous. That's the kind of man to look for, Kathleen, dear—one who has fun with his money." She looked at the Saint again with her keen bright eyes, for the first time as if she were seeing him personally. "And this is a real man, too. I can tell. If I were forty years younger, I'd be after him myself."

"You don't have to be a day younger, Aunt Flo," said the Saint genially. "I'm a charter member of the Chesterfield Club."

The little colour that was in Miss Warshed's face drained out, leaving it a white mask in which the discreetly applied rouge over her cheeks stood out like patches of raw paint. Her lips quivered, and she held on to the table as if to steady herself in her chair, so tightly that even her knuckles and fingertips blanched under the pressure.

"I don't think I quite follow that," she said.

"Oh, hadn't you heard of it?" said the Saint innocently, apparently unaware even of the bewildered way that Kathleen looked from Aunt Flo to him. "Lord Chesterfield was an English pundit who was rated pretty hippy a hundred or two years ago. He gave his name to the sofa but not to the cigarette. He also wrote a series of letters to his son, full of profound advice and wisdom, which were published in book form and bestowed by doting parents on Heaven knows how many other equally bored young men. One of his best remembered tips was that older ladies were the best ones to fall in love with, because they appreciated it so much more. I've always been a rooter for his club for that."

Aunt Flo relaxed quite slowly.

"Indeed." Her lips cracked in a smile, but her eyes were still haunted. "For a moment I simply couldn't imagine what you were talking about. That's very charming. And so true. But I'm sure the young ones already appreciate you more than it's good for you. Are you staying here long?"

"Only a day or two."

"I'm sorry—it was nice meeting you."

She gave him her hand, all graciousness and poise again, and by then it was hard to believe that only a few seconds ago she had seemed to be transfixed with stark terror.

"What on earth is this Chesterfield Club business?" Kathleen demanded as soon as they were at a safe distance.

"You heard me," Simon said. "As a student of all the great philosophers and bores——"

"Don't give me that," she said. "I saw what it did to her when you first mentioned it."

Simon handed over a dollar in exchange for two ice-cream cones which were being practically forced into their hands. He gave his to the first infant that passed, who promptly squashed it on its mother's best afternoon dress.

"You're much too young to remember," said the Saint happily, "but back in the wildest Prohibition days of Kansas City, the Chesterfield Club was an institution that travellers came from all over to see. It was a place where the tired business man could really get a lift with his lunch. All the waitresses were stark naked."

"Oh." Kathleen gulped. "Now I can see why Aunt Flo was shocked."

"Would you say 'shocked' was the word?" Simon asked gently.

He lighted a cigarette and stared through a veil of smoke at the edifying spectacle of a bejewelled dowager leaning over the rail of an enclosure called Fortune's Fish-pond, cane pole in hand, angling with intense concentration for a bottle of Bollinger.

"Even the most sheltered ladies in town at the time must have heard of it," he said. "If a man referred to it in front of them, I can picture them being righteously scandalized, or freezing into the We Are Not Amused re-action. But can you see any of them looking downright terrified, as if the next thing they heard might be the end of the world?"

"But it *couldn't* have meant anything personal to Aunt Flo! I mean——"

"No, not that." He grinned. "I don't think she was ever a waitress at the Chesterfield Club. Even that long ago, she'd've been a bit old for the job."

"Then what do you make of it?"

"You wanted to get me interested," he said, "and you have. How can I meet Brother Powls?"

This could not have been an insuperable problem at the worst; but since it was that kind of charity fair, and Santa Barbara is that kind of place, it proved even easier than he would have anticipated. They were continuing their idle stroll through the grounds, discussing the best pretext they might use for dropping in at Mr Powls' apartment, when Kathleen suddenly clutched Simon's arm.

"Talk of the devil," she said, "there he is—over there, in the light grey jacket."

Mr Alton Powls did not look much like a devil, except as he might be depicted in the more sophisticated modern type of fantasy. From his mildly jaunty Panama hat down to his polished black and white shoes, he looked like a typical member of the county set in which he was imperturbably working for acceptance. His attendance at this garden carnival, properly viewed, was not even surprising at all : on the contrary, it was a social obligation which he could hardly have avoided.

Only the Saint's peculiarly analytic eye would have noted, as they approached on a calculated collision course, a certain revealing shuffle in the way Mr Powls walked, and the no less typical way his glances roved restlessly over a wide area with little corresponding movement of his head.

"Why, good afternoon, Mr Powls," Kathleen said as they met.

He had seen them coming already, but he raised his hat with the most urbane spontaneity.

"Miss Holland. How nice to see you taking a day off."

He was probably not much over sixty, a thin man with a sedate little bulge below his belt. His somewhat lumpy face was clean shaven and pallid, his hair sparse and lank. His lips were tight and gristly, and scarcely moved when he spoke. Simon could see the superficial reasons for describing him as a Creep, but his manner was easy and polite.

Kathleen said : "This is Mr Tem——"

"Templar," said the Saint. He amplified it, very clearly : "Simon Templar."

"Simon Templar," Mr Powls repeated. "Somehow, the name sounds familiar."

His fingers, which had gone out automatically to meet the Saint's cordial hand, lay in the Saint's grasp like cold sausages.

"You could have heard it," Simon said affably.

"You couldn't—by any chance—be any relative of that man they call the Saint?"

"I am the Saint," Simon beamed.

Those who know the Saint at all well will recognize at once that this was totally unlike him. But he did it this time, and Mr Powls retrieved his hand quickly, as if afraid that it might not be given back.

"Are you really?" said Mr Powls. He coughed, to clear a trace of hoarseness from his voice. "But you aren't expecting to find anything to merit your attention here, are you?"

"I never know where I'll find those things," said the Saint cheerfully. "But I'm always on the lookout for them. And there's no place like a town full of respectable retired people. They all buy each other's stories, but who ever checks on them? A guy could come here straight from Leavenworth and give out that he was a retired Bible salesman, and no one would even ask him to prove it by naming the four Gospels."

"That's very interesting," said Mr Powls faintly.

"Not that I think there's anything crooked about this shindig," Simon went on exuberantly. "In fact, it must be on the level, because they just let me win a pot at Bingo. Look."

He pulled out of his pocket the card which he had kept as a souvenir, and thrust it upon Mr Powls in such a way that the other was virtually forced to take it from him.

"That's wonderful," said Mr Powls, returning the card as quickly as he could. "Really, it gives me an inspiration. I must go there and try my luck. If you'll excuse me." He raised his hat to Kathleen again, and inclined his head to the Saint. "Perhaps we'll meet again later."

"I hope so," Simon said heartily. "Let me know if you see any other old lags around."

Mr Powls moved away, not hurriedly, but without looking back.

"I'm getting rather baffled," Kathleen said, "and now I don't think I'm enjoying it."

"You got me started," Simon reminded her. "And I got some results."

"I didn't see much, except that you upset him."

"Does that matter? You said he was a Creep, anyway."

"But you were almost objectionable."

"No. A bit corny and collegiate, maybe. A shade heavy-handed with the humour. But I had to be. I wanted to start something. A respectable citizen may be bored by the kind of kidding that suggests he's an old jailbird, but he isn't offended, because it's too ridiculous to take seriously. Only an old lag would be jolted, because it's too close to home."

"You think he *is* an ex-convict?"

"I've no more doubt about it. But I saw it first in the way he walks and talks and looks around."

"Then why did you go on—the way you did?"

Simon shrugged. His sky-blue eyes were altogether lazy now, and seemed to be ranging perspectives far outside the eucalyptus trees and formal hedges of the manorial grounds which had been turned over to the benefit.

"I'm a catalyst," he said. "You know what that is, in chemistry? You throw a certain catalyst into a certain mixture, and nothing happens to it itself, but all hell breaks loose around it. All the other ingredients seethe up and do back-flips into new transformations. That's me. Half the time I don't have to do anything except be around. Somebody hears I'm the Saint, and I shoot a few arrows in the air, and the fireworks start. Like this. It's no crime to be an ex-convict, unless you got out through a tunnel. Or to be a Creep, even. And I don't know what Aunt Flo is sweating out. So there's nothing much I could do about 'em. And yet I've got an idea that events are already on the march."

She was almost exasperatedly incredulous.

"And now they'll take care of themselves. There must be more to it than that!"

"Well, there may be a little more," he smiled. "Let's go and get a real drink somewhere, and on the way you could show me where Brother Powls lives."

But when they parted later he had still managed to evade being pinned down to anything more positive than a promise to pick her up for lunch the next day.

He was obliged to dine with his friends at their home; but afterwards—having made conversation about everything except the problem with which Kathleen Holland had presented him—he made the excuse of having to take an important letter to the post office to make sure it would go out by the earliest possible mail. He had no such letter and did not even go near the post office, but drove instead to the small new building that Kathleen had shown him, which was pleasantly situated a block from Cabrillo Boulevard within sight of the ocean and the pier and yacht harbour. There was a light in the upper corner that she had pointed out, and he went up the outside stairway and knocked on the door.

Mr Powls opened it, and his jaw dropped.

"What. . . . Yes, Mr Templar. I was hardly expecting——"

"May I come in?" said the Saint, and went in irresistibly.

"What can I do for you, sir?"

"For a start," said the Saint, "you can give me any folding money you've got on you."

He kept one hand deep in his jacket pocket, not being so crude as to stretch it out of shape by making anything point through it, but the suggestion was just as effective to Mr Powls' flickering eyes.

"What is this—a stick-up?"

"Call it what you like, Alton, but sprout the lettuce."

"I think it'd be better if I called the police. You wouldn't shoot me for the few dollars I've got on me."

"Do you remember me making you admire my Bingo card this afternoon, chum?" Simon said. "I did that to get your fingerprints on it. You may not believe it, but I have all sorts of useful connexions—even here. Those prints are already on their way to Washington," he elaborated mendaciously, "only I haven't told anyone yet where they came from. If you feel like calling the police, I won't stop you. By the time we all get to the station there should be a make from the FBI, and we can go on from there."

Mr Powls took a crumpled fold of currency from his trouser pocket and passed it over.

"Nobody ever told me the Saint went in for this kind of thing," he sneered.

"These are rugged days, Alton. What with inflated prices and a confiscatory income tax, it isn't so easy to live like a millionaire any more without a little side money."

"But why pick on me?"

Simon had been scrutinizing each piece of paper money in the roll he had taken and separating it into two slim packs clipped between different fingers. Now he fanned out one sheaf like a poker hand.

"I marked all these bills with two little tears close together near one corner, just before I gave them to Aunt Flo this afternoon as a charity donation. How did you get them?"

"She gave them to me. I was lucky, too."

"You certainly were. But that goes back to when you first hit Santa Barbara and ran into a meal ticket when you were just window-shopping. What were you in stir for, comrade?"

"You'll find out soon enough. It was about some uranium stock I sold. There shouldn't of been any squawk at all, but I wrote something in a letter and they used it to hang a federal rap on me."

"And now you're out, you've switched from the bunco racket to blackmail. That sums it up, doesn't it?"

"You're talking to yourself."

"And even taking it out of charity donations."

"She gave it to me," Powls repeated. "I don't know where it came from. If she snitched it where she shouldn't, what does that make her?"

"A scared old lady," said the Saint. "What have you got on her?"

Mr Powls' cartilaginous lips curled. He was regaining confidence quickly.

"I should tell you—so that you can take over. You dig that up for yourself, if you're so wise. You can't beat it out of me here, without one of the neighbours'll call the cops, and you don't want that any more than I do. Leave me alone to handle it, and I might even give you a little cut."

The Saint's smile was terribly benevolent.

"I'm only humanly inquisitive about Aunt Flo," he said. "But I'm just as humanly certain that whatever her guilty secret is she's done a great job of living it down for twenty years. And you should have heard that blackmail is one of the crimes I rate among the wickedest in the world and among the least adequately punished by the law."

He held Mr Alton Powls by the coat lapel and shook him back and forth quite gently, while the forefinger of his other hand tapped him on the chest for emphasis; and

his eyes were sword-points of sapphire in the angelic kindliness of his face.

"I shall give you twelve hours to get out of Santa
Barbara, and a few more to be out of the state of California," he said. "And if I run into you after that, the only
cut I shall take will be in your throat."

He went out without a backward glance.

He got into his car and drove purposefully away, knowing full well that he was watched from the window above;
but after four blocks he circled around and came quietly
down an alley to coast to a stop with his lights out in its
blackest patch of shadow from which he could watch the
building he had just left.

When Mr Powls came out a few minutes later, and
drove off in a small car from an open garage under one
end of the building, Simon did not even have to be cau-
tious about following him. Unburdened with luggage of
any kind, Mr Powls was certainly not rushing to beat the
liberal deadline he had been given. There was only one
place where he could have been headed, other than the
one which could have been generically described as Out of
There, and Simon set his own course for it by another
route.

If the Saint had not been quite so confident about it, it
is barely possible that Mr Alton Powls might be alive today. Simon knew the address of the Warshed ménage,
which was available to anyone who could read a telephone
directory; and having ascertained that, he had not
bothered to ask Kathleen Holland to show it to him. He
thought he knew his way around the Montecito district
fairly well, and he had driven a score of times over the
road on which their house stood. The one thing he had
overlooked was that he had only driven over it and not
in search of a specific destination on it; and he had temporarily forgotten the penchant of denizens of even less

traditionally aloof areas than this for secreting their street numbers in minuscule figures in the obscurest possible location, whether to discourage process servers or poor relations. Thus he made two abortive passes at his target, each time made slower by the fact that he did not want to arrive with a triumphant roar, before he positively identified the right entrance. And then he had to drift two hundred yards past it, and find a wider place in the road to park, before he could walk back and enter the rustic gates on foot.

By which time, perhaps, Mr Alton Powls had already been gathered to his fathers, if an overworked recording angel could put the finger on them.

At any rate, he looked dead enough, as the Saint saw him after threading a catlike way to the house which stood completely secluded from the road within its ramparts of tall clipped hedges—after circumnavigating Mr Powls' small car which by this time was cooling in the driveway, and high-stepping delicately over odorous flower beds, and almost falling into a treacherous excavation in the middle of a small patch of lawn, and finally reaching the draped living-room window from which the light came, and selecting the one marginal crack in the curtains through which he could steal the widest wedge-shaped view of the interior.

Mr Alton Powls was dead on the carpet, with blood welling from a dent in his cranium, and Aunt Flo standing over him with a poker in her hand, and the two comparatively junior Misses observing the scene with respectful approbation.

In contravention of all the time-honoured legends about old maids, the french windows were not even latched. Simon opened them at once, and made an inevitably sensational entrance through the drapes which wrung stifled screams from Violet and Ida. Only Aunt Flo stood silent and undaunted.

"I'm very sorry," he said. "This is entirely my fault."

"What are we to understand by that, Mr Templar?—he told us your real name."

"I knew he was blackmailing you, but I was curious to know how. The easiest way to find out seemed to be to follow him here and eavesdrop a little. But when I started the routine that I figured would make him come here, I didn't know that I'd have the answer even before he arrived. I picked his pocket just before I left him a few minutes ago, and here's what I found when I had a chance to look."

He produced Mr Powls' wallet and unfolded a newspaper clipping from it, which he had read under a shielded flashlight while he waited in the alley. It could only be the same clipping which Kathleen Holland had described Mr Powls exhibiting in *Ye Needle Nooke*. It was from the Kansas City *Star*, under a 1930 dateline, and described a raid on one of the most elegant local brothels. There was also a picture of some of the principal culprits being arraigned in night court. The accused madam was plainly identified as Florence Warshed, and the likeness was unmistakable even after more than a quarter-century. Among the other girls, less easily recognizable, were two others modestly named as Violet Smith and Ida Jones.

Simon handed the clipping to Aunt Flo, who barely glanced at it and let Ida take it and pass it to Violet.

"I thought you'd like to burn it yourselves," said the Saint.

Aunt Flo had not let go the poker, but her grip was perceptibly less rigid.

"I've heard that you're a man who might understand some things that ordinary people wouldn't," she said steadily. "I always ran a good house, if you know what I mean. But after Repeal I could see the handwriting on the wall. I could afford to retire. Violet and Ida were getting a bit too old for the best clients, and yet it wasn't a good time for them to take over a house on their own. They'd been with me longest of all my girls—in fact, they might just as well have been my own nieces. When the time came, we found that none of us wanted to split up and go it alone. After all, we didn't have any place to go—we were the only real family any of us had left. So we decided to stick together. We got in my car and headed west, and soon after we found this town we knew it was for us. We could settle down and nobody would ever dream we'd ever been any different from all we wanted to be from there on."

"You only made one slip that might have started me wondering, before I tried you on the Chesterfield Club," Simon remarked with incurably professional acuity. "The slant you all have about people being good spenders. But not many people would notice it—and you were right, this is one of the last places in the country where you'd be likely to run into an old client. Even that mightn't've been fatal—most pillars of this community would be too worried about whether you'd keep your mouth shut to open their own. But it had to be this Alton Powls."

"He was always a cheap grifter and I'd be ashamed to class him with my good clients," said Aunt Flo. "But after he had the luck to spot us, and even went back and dug up that newspaper article to make sure he could rub it in, he's been taking us for a hundred dollars a week."

Simon nodded.

"Kathleen guessed he was giving you trouble, but she was only worried about you. She thinks you're wonderful, and so do I. So I took it upon myself to give him my best warning, to lay off you and chisel his chips somewhere else. I was betting that this would send him hustling right over here to put the last big bite on you, but I was planning to be in the wings myself."

He bent and examined what was left of Mr Powls more conscientiously, for pulse and heartbeat, of which he verified that there were neither.

"He phoned and said he had to see us at once," Aunt Flo related. "Then when he got here he told us something about you calling on him. He wanted to see our bank books—he said we'd have to draw out every cent we could raise and give it to him before he left in the morning. And then we could get a mortgage on this place, which would take longer, and send him some more when he wrote to us."

"That's what I expected."

"The girls were trying to talk him out of it, but I knew he'd never lay off as long as he lived, so I picked up the poker and fixed that," said Aunt Flo defiantly, but her voice broke for the first time.

The Saint took the poker from her without resistance, wiped it carefully on Mr Powls' neat grey jacket, and put it back in the fireplace.

"I'd probably have done the same thing myself, if I'd got here in time," he said. "Or something like it. There are only three ways to stop a blackmailer, but only fools go on paying him, and it would be asking too much for you to dare him to tell the worst. . . . I noticed an interesting hole in your lawn as I was sneaking up on you. Did you have any plans for it?"

"We were getting ready to plant a Chinese elm," said Aunt Flo wistfully. "Quite a large and expensive one, but we needed more shade for the fuchsias."

"I'm afraid you'll just have to make it another flower bed now," said the Saint sympathetically. He searched for Mr Powls' keys and thoughtfully took possession of them before he picked up the body. "I won't try to cover him very deeply tonight, because I'll have to run back to his apartment and pack up all his personal things to bury with him, so that it'll look as if he simply blew town for mysterious reasons of his own. Also the people I'm staying with are expecting me back, and I can't stretch a story about a flat tyre too far. But I'll be here first thing in the morning with some plants from a nursery, and make a slap-up job of it. Why don't you all go to bed and get a good sleep?"

The account he gave Kathleen Holland the next day of his final interview with Mr Alton Powls was not fundamentally fictitious, but it took advantage of certain major omissions.

"I don't think we should pry too hard into Aunt Flo's awful secret," he said. "It probably isn't anything that'd scare anybody but her, anyhow. All I know is that I put the fear of God into your creepy friend, and if you drop by his apartment this afternoon I bet you'll find he's already done a flit."

Having left Mr Powls' car parked near the railroad station, he was prepared to let any other perfunctory inquirers take the trail from there.

"I almost feel let down," Kathleen said disappointedly. "I was half hoping you'd do something brilliant and discover that he was Violet and Ida's black-sheep father."

"If I had, I wouldn't even tell you," said the Saint darkly. "And don't even hint to Aunt Flo that I've talked to you at all. It would only worry her. But between you and me, I stopped at her house this morning and told her who I was and that I was sure she wouldn't have any more trouble."

"You looked so hot when you got here," Kathleen said,

"I thought you'd been doing something much more violent than that."

"Believe it or not," said the Saint complacently, "before I was through she had me with a spade in my hands working like a bloody grave-digger. I tell you, I get into the damnedest things."

The Element of Doubt

"The Law is a wonderful thing, I suppose," Simon Templar said in one of his oracular moods. "I've done a lot of complaining about it in my time, but if it had never existed I wouldn't have had all the fun of breaking it. And it's probably a very fine idea that all the wretched little people who can't take care of themselves should be able to get a fair shake. The trouble is that the same machinery that prevents injustice can also prevent justice."

He could be more specific about this if anybody wanted to listen :

"If you want to guarantee a man the benefit of any reasonable doubt, you also get a system with built-in loopholes that a sufficiently cunning lawyer can drive a bus through. And then you'll have a certain number of lawyers who specialize in doing just that—who don't give a damn how guilty they know their clients are as long as they can pay the bill. In fact, who'd rather defend a man who's guilty as hell, because the fee can be so much fatter. There's a lot of boils on the cosmos alive and free today who'd be behind bars or under a slab if it weren't for that kind of shyster. Sometimes I think those professional cheaters of the Law should be hanged even higher than their customers."

The Saint did not have to mention what he had done himself to remedy some of the failures of formal jurisprudence, for by that time quite as much as was safe for him was already known about his freewheeling interpretation of justice.

In those days, Mr Carlton Rood was an outstanding example of the type of attorney whose neck might have been in frequent jeopardy if the Saint's heterodox theories of legal responsibility had prevailed in the statute books.

From the foundation of his first two spectacular acquittals had been built up a reputation for court-room invincibility that had become a legend of his generation. It was a legend that enjoyed some of the advantages of a chain reaction, for every successful defence could be counted on to draw new crops of desperate defendants to his office, and by this date it had reached a point where in any *cause* sufficiently *célèbre* it was almost mandatory to retain Carlton Rood. Among his grateful clients could be listed some of the biggest names that ever adorned a theatre marquee or a police dossier, and there is no doubt that they all received value for their money.

If there were any tricks of delay, confusion, objection, and obfuscation which Mr Rood did not know, nobody else had ever thought of them either. On the principle that no case was lost until the last appeal had failed, he approached every assignment with a dazzling variety of technical devices primarily designed to postpone any irrevocable result to the remotest possible future, before which prosecutors could lose their steam, judges could grow numb with boredom, and inconvenient witnesses could be overtaken by clouding of the memory or simply die of old age—if not otherwise helped off the scene by interested parties. But when in spite of all shenanigans he was brought to a showdown, he had no peer in the forensic techniques and pyrotechnics of leading, misleading, tripping, trapping, twisting, bamboozling, pleading, bullying, hand-wringing, gamut-running, and plain ham acting that can be employed to obscure an issue or distort a fact.

He was a heavy-set heavy-featured man with a luxurious growth of silver hair which he cultivated to the proportions of a mane. The combination gave him a leonine and statesmanlike aspect of which he was fully aware and which he exploited to the utmost, enhancing them with the gold-rimmed pince-nez dangling on a wide black ribbon, the string ties, and the dark clothes of slightly old-fashioned cut which are part of the stock cartoon of a Southern senator. On him they looked right and extraordinarily impressive, so that the most hostile jury usually ended up listening to him with respect, in spite of the sceptical attitude which his own publicity had inspired in large cynical sections of the population, which inclined to the view that anyone who went to the expense of hiring Carlton Rood should be presumed guilty until irrefutably proved otherwise.

The verdict in Mr Rood's latest headline trial was being awaited hourly on a certain day when Simon stopped in Biloxi on the Gulf Coast for gas. While he was waiting for his tank to be filled, he saw a newspaper van pull up at a tiny shop next door while the driver delivered a bundle of papers. Simon walked over and went in as the van drove away, and found a stout middle-aged woman fumbling with the string that held the package together.

"Can I help you?" he said gallantly.

He deftly loosened the knot, and turned over the top paper. The black type leaped to his eye like a blow :

SHOLTO ACQUITTED

It was a result that the Saint would have bet considerable odds against, but for once his gift of prophecy must have succumbed to wishful thinking. Carlton Rood had done it again. But the achievement was so startling that Simon was conscious of suppressing a gasp, and may not have completely succeeded.

"Did he get off?" asked the woman.

She was looking right across the newspaper when she spoke, and Simon suddenly understood why she wore dark glasses in spite of the gloom inside the shop.

"I'm afraid so," he said gently. "Would you like to know all the grisly details?"

"Thank you, but my niece'll read it to me when she gets here from school. It doesn't really matter how he did it, if he got off. I thought this might be one time when he wouldn't, but I suppose that was too much to hope. I *have* been hoping it, though—ever since he blinded me."

She said this in such a matter-of-fact tone that he wondered momentarily if one or the other of them had slipped a cog.

"How was that?" he prompted cautiously.

"Oh, it was nearly twelve years ago, when he was still doing some of his own dirty work. They might have got him for murder then, if it hadn't been for what happened to me. You probably read about it at the time. My name's Agnes Yarrow."

Although there was little criminal news that he had missed since he began to make a notable amount of it himself, and his memory was prodigious, he would have had to admit that he could not always recall everything that had ever happened in the annals of gangsterism from a single reference. But the blind woman quickly relieved him of the need to ply her with questions.

"My husband and I had a small dry cleaning business in Mobile. Sholto was organizing a Laundry and Cleaning Association, as he called it. It was just a racket for him to get ten per cent of everybody's business, but he let you know that if you didn't sign up with the Association you wouldn't have any business. We were the first to refuse to join. One day Sholto came in and started spraying acid out of a flit gun over all the clothes that were waiting to be picked up. I tried to stop him, and I got a squirt of acid in my face. I fell down screaming, and my husband came out of the back room and grabbed him. He took the flit gun away from him and he would have held him, he was a big strong man, but Sholto pulled out a gun and shot him dead and ran away."

"But he was arrested later, and—— Yes, I remember now. Carlton Rood defended him. It was one of his first important successes. But now it comes back, it seems to me that Sholto wasn't even tried for murder, only for the attack on you."

"That's right: I still don't understand it all, but the District Attorney seemed to get an idea that if he could convict him of the attack first, it'd be much easier to convict him of murder afterwards. But if they couldn't, they'd save the expense of a much bigger trial."

"A fascinating idea," said the Saint. "I wonder if Carlton Rood helped to give it to him."

"I don't know. But Sholto got off. He had some sort of alibi, and they couldn't find anyone who'd seen him leaving the shop. I was the only one who could have identified him—and I'd lost my sight. Of course, I'd heard his voice, too, but that's much harder. His attorney made a complete fool of me in court when it came to picking out his voice from a lot of others."

Simon nodded.

"That seems to ring a bell. He had private detectives with tape recorders all over the country, scouting for people with voices like Sholto's. He even hired professional mimics. It was one of the tricks that made him famous."

"It worked, anyhow," Mrs Yarrow said with a kind of weary resignation. "It was months afterwards, and you don't remember a voice the same as you do a face, at least not when you're more used to relying on your eyes."

"But you're absolutely sure, in your own mind, that it was Sholto?"

"I was absolutely certain, the first time the police let me hear him talk. It was only afterwards that the lawyers confused me. And it must have been him, mustn't it? Look at everything he's done since."

The Saint could not bring himself to point out that this argument was the direct antithesis of some of the fundamental tenets of civilized legal doctrine, for it was an attitude which he had often taken himself.

Instead, he said : "Isn't there any chance of doing anything for your eyes?"

"Nothing. They told me before I left the hospital that I'd never see again."

"But that was a long time ago," he persisted. "Haven't you tried again since?"

She shook her head.

"I don't see any use trying to keep giving myself false hopes. They were much too definite. And I've learned to live with it. But I still can't stop wishing Sholto would get what he deserves."

Simon paid for the paper and went back to the car which he seemed to have left in another chapter of his existence, so much had changed since he walked into the little sundries store.

It was not really such a wild coincidence that he had thus met Mrs Yarrow and heard her story, for at the time he had not been personally preoccupied with either Rood or Sholto. Although he could visualize them as theoretically intriguing subjects for future attention, his interest at the moment had been only the lively but abstract interest of any wide-awake citizen, which would also have encompassed the latest Hollywood marriage or the latest South American revolution. It would have been no more important a coincidence, mathematically, if the news vendor had turned out to have once manicured the film star or nursed the deposed President or had any distant connection with anyone else in the news. The difference was that in any other such situation the Saint would have murmured some polite clichés and quickly forgotten the whole thing. Agnes Yarrow fell into another category only because this was the kind of encounter which so often brought the Saint's catholic but diffused concern for the Ungodly into sharp focus on one or two particular specimens.

Mr Carlton Rood, as a result of such an accidental conversation, was suddenly promoted into this inauspicious spotlight.

Simon Templar travelled no farther that day than one of the motels facing the Gulf west of town, where he read the complete newspaper story and then spent two or three hours in intense meditation. The stratagems by which Mr Rood had won another acquittal for his client need not be retold here in laborious detail: it is sufficient for this story, as it was for the Saint's motivation, that they were typically ingenious, immoral, and successful. Nothing else was needed to qualify Mr Rood for immediate retribution, in the Saint's judgment; but the manner of providing for it required inventiveness and planning.

After dinner that night he made a long-distance phone call, and the next morning he drove back to Biloxi and Mrs Yarrow's little shop.

"I took what you may think was rather a liberty last night," he told her. "I talked about your case to a friend of mine in Santa Barbara, California, who's one of the best ophthalmologists in the country. I must tell you bluntly that he wasn't very optimistic. But he would like to see you."

"It's very kind of you," she said. "But I just can't afford a trip like that."

"I'd like to pay for it—please don't be offended. If that sounds too much like charity, I promise that if he is able to restore your sight I'll let you pay me back every penny. I know you'd think that was worth the money. But if he can't do anything for you it won't cost you a cent. Let me take the gamble, and I give you my word it won't hurt my bank account a bit if I lose."

"But I told you I didn't want to torment myself with false hopes."

"You want something done about Sholto, don't you? If you had your sight back, you could identify him again —and he could still be tried for the murder of your husband. That would mean something to you, wouldn't it?"

As she wavered, he took her hand and put an envelope into it.

"This is a plane ticket I bought this morning, in your name, from New Orleans to Santa Barbara," he said. "The reservation is for Sunday—that gives you three days to make your personal arrangements, and it should be a good day for you to get someone to drive you to the airport. You have to change planes in Los Angeles, but the airline will look after you there. And I'll have my doctor friend send someone to meet you at Santa Barbara airport. His name and address are written on the envelope, if you want to tell your friends where you're going."

"But what about *your* name?" she protested weakly. "And why do you want to do this for me? I don't know anything about you except that you've got a nice voice!"

"That's all I intend you to know right now," said the Saint. "But if you must think of me by some label, you may call me Santa Claus."

He drove to New Orleans himself the same morning and took the next plane to New York, where Mr Rood had long since transferred his headquarters from his more pastoral beginning in the South.

One of the Saint's intangible assets, and one of incalculable value in his peculiar activities, was the vast and variegated collection of acquaintances that he had accumulated and cultivated over the years, a roster of trades and professions that was a unique classified directory in itself. Besides a friend who was a distinguished ophthalmologist he could have produced with equal facility an ophicleidist, an oil rigger, or, probably, an orang-outang. Another man whose talents he needed lived in New York when not working elsewhere, and Simon was fortunate to find him at liberty.

In the course of the following week, Mr Rood received certain visitors at his office whose rôles in his destiny he did not perceive.

The first was a new client who sought his advice about making a will which would distribute his fortune fairly among his wife and daughters, protect them from fortune-hunters, ensure a substantial inheritance for his still unborn grandchildren, and yet not leave his heirs under a state of absolute tutelage. Mr Rood discoursed for some time on the theoretical problems involved, until he learned that about 99% of the million-dollar estate which the man was so worried about was contingent on his successful marketing of the idea of making automobiles impervious to minor collisions by building the bodies entirely out of soft rubber. Whereupon Mr Rood briskly recommended him to consult first with a patent attorney, and never thought about him again.

The second caller presented himself as a free-lance journalist who specialized in writing autobiographies, speeches, or any other kind of material for celebrities who were, if not otherwise unqualified, too busy for the dull toil of capturing their scintillating thoughts in page after page of readable prose. If he could not name any names whom he had served in this capacity, he could claim this reticence as proof of his inviolable discretion : part of his service was to avert even the slight stigma of the "as told to" type of by-line, and those who wanted to claim his articles as their own original work could do so without fear that any other person would ever hear who really wrote them. Reassuringly, he was asking nothing more than permission to approach certain editors with the idea of a series of the great lawyer's reminiscences of his famous cases ; if the work was commissioned, Mr Rood would simply supply him with court records and spend a few hours talking them over, and of course the finished stories would be completely subject to Mr Rood's editing and approval. It was an unexceptionally straightforward-sounding proposition, and Mr Rood was quite interested in discussing it. The Saint could be disarmingly flattering and persuasive when he tried, even when wearing a rumpled suit and a studious-looking pair of horn-rimmed glasses and using the undistinguished name of Tom Simons.

After their talk had reached an encouraging stage of warmth and relaxation, the Saint was able to say in the most spontaneous conversational manner :

"One thing I've often wondered about, Mr Rood. Aren't you ever afraid that some of your ex-clients might start worrying about you as a sort of security risk ?"

"Good heavens, no !" responded the advocate, in genuine astonishment. "They were all innocent men, wrongfully accused, and so proven by due process of law, as the records show."

"Naturally. But many of them were at least generally rumoured, shall we say, to have been involved in some rather dubious activities aside from the crimes they were actually charged with. In preparing their defence, you may easily have had access to a lot of incidental informa-tion about other associations or misbehaviours which could be very embarrassing for them if you talked too much."

"That might be true. But an ethical lawyer's confidence is as sacred as the confessional."

"The underworld doesn't put much faith in lofty principles," said the Saint. "I must be a little more frank. Because of my job, I have some rather peculiar contacts. The other day I happened to mention you and the idea we've been discussing to a man whom of course I can't name, who has some rather special connections of his own. He told me he'd heard that some big fellows were wondering if you weren't getting to know too much for your own good, and that you mightn't be around so much longer."

Mr Rood rubbed his chin.

"That's an extraordinary notion. I can think of no reason why anyone would doubt me."

"But of course you've taken precautions, just in case some trigger-happy mobster got ideas."

"What sort of precautions?" asked the attorney guardedly.

"Like making a list of the men most likely to worry about you, with some notes on the reasons why, and leaving it in safe hands with instructions to deliver it to the police if you should die of anything but the most incontestably natural causes, and dropping a tactful word in the right places about what you've done."

"Oh, that, obviously," said Mr Rood, in a tone which betrayed to Simon's hypersensitive ear that the thought had just begun to commend itself.

The Saint had achieved his object, and there was no point in prolonging the interview.

"Then I won't worry about being able to finish this job, once we get it started," he said cheerfully, and stood up.

"I hope I'll have some news for you in a week or two. And thanks for sparing me so much of your valuable time."

"You have a very interesting proposition, Mr Simons," said Carlton Rood heartily, shaking his hand with a large and adhesive paw. "I'll look forward to hearing more from you."

Yet another visitor came late that night, by-passing the janitor and climbing ten flights of emergency stairs to unlock the office through a neat hole cut in the glass upper panel of the entrance door. This visitor broke into several filing cabinets and strewed their contents over the floor, but did not try to tackle the massive safe in which all really important papers were kept. He took nothing except about $200 which he found in the petty cash box—the Saint could be munificently generous when he chose, but could never resist the smallest tax-free contribution towards his non-deductible expenses when it could be taken from the right coffers.

Mr Rood was not unduly perturbed by this minor larceny and vandalism, but nevertheless it aggravated an irksome hangnail of dubiety which had been scuffed up by the affable "Tom Simons". And he was enough of a believer in symbols to take it as a direct providential nudge to procrastinate no longer over the simple practical suggestion that had been made to him. He cancelled a dinner engagement the next night, and spent the evening at work on a highly inflammable document intended only for posthumous publication.

Long before that, Simon Templar had telephoned Santa Barbara again.

"She seems to be doing all right," said his friend. "But it will still be three or four days before we know if we have any luck. Don't count on it too much. I told you that the chance was very small."

"But not hopeless."

"No, not hopeless, or I would not have operated. You must try to be patient."

"You know that isn't my long suit, Mickey. However—did everything else go according to plan?"

"Yes, just as we talked about it. I was able to move her from the hospital yesterday, in Georgia's car, so they don't know where she went, and in the private nursing home she has another name, under which I opened a separate file in my office records, so there is no trace of the connection."

"Thanks, pal," said the Saint. "Take care to keep it that way. For the time being, her life may depend on it."

By the time Mr Rood embarked on his secret literary endeavour, the Saint had flown back to New Orleans, reclaimed his car at the airport, and taken the road to Atlanta, where the beneficiary of Mr Rood's latest legal triumph made his home. Simon was not only temperamentally short on patience, but he had even less inclination to let an act of justice that he had decided upon teeter on the outcome of a medical long shot of which the surgeon himself was less than optimistic about the result.

Joseph Sholto, enjoying the expansive euphoria induced by a narrow escape of which even he had been far from confident, would at this moment have guffawed hysterically at any suggestion that he would ever doubt the maxim which had been one of the guiding principles of his adult career, that a bad boy's best friend is his lawyer.

Joe Sholto (to the initiated he was more generally known as "Dibs") had come a long way since he was doing his own strong-arm and squirt-gun work to try to put over a protection racket on Mobile's laundries and dry cleaners. When he had achieved enough limited success to be noticed, he received the standard accolade from the Syndicate: come in or get out. Prudently, Dibs decided to sell, but kept his own independence; when he came in, he wanted to be as an equal, not as one of a host of minor hangers-on. He had his ups and downs, but thanks to a ruthless devotion to his own welfare and his faith in the best legal chicanery he managed to avoid any disastrous collisions with constitutional justice, so that he became one of those semi-mythological names which are vaguely known to the public and baldly referred to by the press as "gangsters" without ever having suffered a major conviction.

He hit the jackpot when he saw the possibilities of the trading stamp business. At this time the craze for these miniature coupons was booming from coast to coast, and probably half the families in America were daily pasting up "stamps" of various colours and designs, given to them by local merchants at the rate of ten for every dollar they spent, in booklets which when filled and accumulated in sufficient numbers could be exchanged for almost anything from a razor to a refrigerator. These stamps were offered to the stores as a merchandising gimmick by a number of reputable firms which also undertook to redeem them, and the competition between them was simply to offer the most attractive premiums at the best price.

One day it dawned upon Dibs Sholto that he too could have a part of this business. The investment in printing the stamps and the booklets to stick them in was relatively trivial, and the goods they would eventually be exchanged for could be bought out of the money the storekeepers would pay for the stamps. It seemed like such a magnificently automatic way of multiplying mazuma that he was slightly disgusted with himself for not having thought of it ten years before. The only trouble now was that the best potential customers, if they were interested at all, had already been signed up by the old-established stamp firms, or in the case of some chains had even set up their own stamp systems.

Again he was too wise to begin by tussling with giants, but there were plenty of pygmies who could be taken for an impressive total poundage. The beauty of the stamp scheme was that it was not limited to any type of sale or service : theoretically, every single shop in every town and village could use them to attract new customers or keep old ones. Yet it was still true that in spite of the wide spread of the craze a majority of smaller enterprises had not succumbed to it, feeling that their modest business did not need or could not afford such promotion. It was in these small tradesmen that Sholto saw his market ; and the smaller they were the more likely they were to succumb to the kind of salesmanship in which he specialized, which offered the cogent inducements of freedom from broken windows, slashed tyres, stink bombs, and even personal injury.

Thus with the encouragement of some property damage and a few salutary beatings, Dibs Sholto's gaudily coloured Double Dividend Stamps throve and spread over the southeast corner of the country until they were as familiar as any other brand to the housewives of five states, most of whom had no notion whatever of how some of the merchants they dealt with had been persuaded to feature them. Being, unlike a barefaced protection racket, an ostensibly legitimate enterprise, the Double Dividend organization managed to escape the monopolistic attention of the criminal hierarchy, and was able to handle local complaints at the county level : there were surprisingly few of these, for Sholto's small sales force of goons were trained to select the prospects most likely to be terrorized. It was Double Dividend's own successful expansion which had brought the first serious trouble on itself. A Congressional Committee nosing into the trading stamp business in general had heard some evidence, an Attorney General had been prodded to take action, and Sholto had found himself on trial in Washington on the federal charges from which it had taken all Carlton Rood's genius to extricate him.

But now that that briefly disconcerting obstacle had been disposed of, Dibs Sholto could see nothing to stop him enlarging his stamp system into a nation-wide network from which the dividends to himself would be not double but tenfold.

"Next time, the big boys won't tell me—they'll ask me," he said to himself. "And they'll make the deal *I* want. I'm on top of something that's all mine, and nobody in the world has a thing on me."

In this mood of resurgent arrogance after a fright which had shaken him more than he would ever admit now to anyone, he was discussing plans for the future with two of his chief lieutenants in the stately Colonial mansion north of the city of Atlanta which he had made his residence, when the white-haired Negro butler who was part of the expensive scenery announced an uninvited visitor.

"Who the hell is Sam Temple?" Sholto wanted to know.

Since no one could tell him, he sent one of his aides to find out. In a few minutes the man came back with an answer.

"He's a two-bit private eye, but he says he ain't here to ask questions—he's got something to sell."

Simon Templar never needed such crude accessories as a false beard to create a character, when he thought there was little danger of being recognized by his features. Merely by plastering his hair down with odorous oil, leaving his shoes unshined, and putting on the same soiled shirt that he had worn all the previous day, with the addition of a garish tie, a pair of loud and clashing socks, and a large diamond ring, all bought at the same dime store, and a little grime under his fingernails, he struck exactly the right note of seedy flashiness; and his manner as he entered Sholto's presence was a convincing blend of obsequiousness and bluster.

"You won't be sorry you saw me, Dibs. What I've got to sell is worth plenty, but I'm not going to make this a stick-up. I'd rather have you feeling you still owed me something than drive a hard bargain. Some other time I might want to ask *you* for a favour, if you know what I mean."

"What're you selling?" Sholto growled.

He was a rather short rotund man with a snub-nosed face which he consciously tried to make less porcine by carrying his chin stuck out at an angle of permanent challenge, and the same crude aggressiveness was duplicated by his habitual voice. But his small shoe-button eyes were coldly calculating and as unemotional as marbles.

"It's like this," said the Saint. "A couple of nights ago I broke into a lawyer's office in New York. I can tell you that because I know it won't go any farther, after we get through talking. A client had hired me to find out if a certain thing was in his files, and you can't be too fussy how you go about a job like that, if you know what I mean."

"Who was this lawyer?"

"Mr Carlton Rood, Dibs—your own mouthpiece, according to what I read in the papers. That's why I'm here now. But what I was looking for didn't have anything to do with you. Only while I was looking, I found a recording machine in his desk which he can turn on if he wants to record a conversation. So I sat down and played the tape that was in it, in case it had anything on it about my client, or anything else that might be useful, if you know what I mean."

"I know what you mean," Sholto snarled. "So what did you hear?"

"There was this piece about you, Dibs. And I knew you'd be interested. So I found a spare spool of tape and made a copy of it—that was easy, machines like that being part of my business, if you know what I mean, and it didn't tip him off like it would if I'd taken the original tape. But you know his voice, and I thought you'd like to hear it."

Simon opened the small attaché case he had brought in with him, whose purpose now became apparent : with the lid off, it proved to be a portable tape recorder and playback. At a nod from Sholto, one of the lieutenants helped him to plug in the cord. There was no longer any problem of piquing the interest of the audience.

The Saint twiddled a couple of knobs, and suddenly the opulent accents of Carlton Rood boomed with startling realism from the instrument :

"*You say that Mrs Yarrow has already been operated on?*"

Then another voice, commonplace but incisive : "*Almost a week ago. The operation was completely successful. In a few weeks she'll have normal vision, and could be called to identify the man who squirted acid at her in Mobile.*"

Rood's florid tones again : "*But that case was thrown out twelve years ago.*"

"*Sholto was never tried for shooting the husband. And there's no statute of limitations on murder.*"

"*But what extraordinary lengths to go to—to revive an ancient case like that——*"

"*The Senator's determined to get Sholto. And several other big scalps. He figures he needs them for his next election campaign. He's paying for all this out of his own pocket and he can afford to.*"

"*Indeed. But why are you telling me this, Mr Simons?*"

"*The Senator is a practical man. In politics, if you can't lick 'em, you join 'em—within limits, of course. The Senator would rather have you on his side than have to fight you. You know how ambitious he is, and he wants this very badly. Here's what I'm authorized to offer. Three hundred thousand dollars cash for all the information and leads you can supply, which of course will never be attributed to you—and it can be handled so as to make it tax free. And a Federal judgeship, which will give you a distinguished peak to retire from in a few years and a perfect out from having to turn down defending your old clients.*"

The Saint gave a quick twist of one finger and thumb, and the sound stopped abruptly.

Sholto glared at him.

"What did you do that for?"

"I think that's plenty for a sample," Simon answered. "I know you want to know what Mr Rood said, but I've got to leave myself something to sell, if you know what I mean."

One of the lieutenants moved menacingly closer, and Simon looked him in the eye and ostentatiously took his hand off the machine.

"Don't be hasty," he said. "You've heard all I brought with me. The rest is on another tape, in a safe place."

Shalto's teeth clamped down on his cigar.

"How much?"

"It should be worth ten grand, easily."

"To hear Rood tell this jerk to tell his Senator to go take a running jump at himself?" Sholto scoffed. "What kind of sucker d'you take me for?"

"I'm not telling you what he says. That's the part you have to pay for."

"And if all you're selling is a false alarm, you know how sorry you'd be?"

"You won't get it out of me that way, Dibs," said the Saint with a thin smile. "But I'm taking the risk that you won't think you were gypped when you've heard it." He paused. "Besides, if we do business, I'm hoping to sell you something else."

"What's that?"

"I expect you'll want to know where this Mrs Yarrow is. Confidential investigations are my business. I could help you find her—for a little extra, that is. But you won't be disappointed. I guarantee I could locate her in less than four days, because of something you haven't heard yet, if you know what I mean."

The racketeer's eyes stayed on him unblinking, expressionless beads of jet, for a long count of seconds, while his stubby fingers beat a mechanical tattoo on his knee. But behind that impenetrable stare Simon knew that an exceptionally shrewd brain was working, for even in the brutal jungles of Dibs Sholto's world a man does not rise to eminence who is slow to grasp and react.

There was obviously no doubt in Sholto's mind about the genuineness of the tape record. And Simon had not for a moment anticipated that there would be, for the friend in New York who had made it for him—after an hour's first-hand study of Mr Rood's vocal mannerisms during an abortive discussion of a problem in willing a million-dollar estate—had in the heyday of radio been one of the most sought-after multi-voiced actors, and was now a professional mimic who made a fairly steady living in the secondary night-club circuit with an act in which he impersonated sundry celebrities. It was a poetic touch that the Saint could never have resisted, to hook Joe Sholto with a similar trick to one of those that Carlton Rood had used twelve years ago to get him off. And from that point Simon felt he could almost hear the turning of cog-wheels behind Sholto's inscrutable scowl.

"I'll have to think it over," Sholto said at last. As Simon shrugged and stood up, he went on : "No, you can stick around. It'll take a while, but not that long." He jerked his cigar at his second lieutenant. "Take him in the dining-room, Earl. Buy him a drink."

Earl opened the door, and Simon followed him docilely across the hall into a room on the other side. There was an assortment of bottles on the sideboard, among which Simon noticed the label of Peter Dawson.

"Help yourself," Earl said hospitably.

He raked together a pack of cards that were scattered over one end of the table, and riffled them thoughtfully.

"You play gin rummy?"

"Not very well," said the Saint modestly.

Joe Sholto was already dialling Long Distance to give the number of one of his special representatives who worked out of Biloxi, and had the good luck to catch him at his office, which was a local pool room.

"Look for a Mrs Agnes Yarrow, who's been living down there," Sholto said. "Find out if she's in town or where she's gone—anything else you can pick up. Call me back right away."

The next number he asked for was in New York, and presently it brought the sonorous tones of Carlton Rood over the wire.

"Good afternoon, Joseph."

"Hiya, Carl." Sholto's voice had all the bluff bonhomie his abrasive disposition could put into it. "I hear you had burglars. . . . Yeah, one of my boys saw it in the paper. Hope you didn't lose anything important. . . . Well, that's too bad, but it could of been worse. Two hundred bucks you can put on the next sucker's bill—but it better not be mine !"

So Rood's office had indeed been broken into—that much of the story checked. They talked for a while about divers loose ends and lesser upshots of the recent trial, and the conversation had about run its natural course when Sholto casually tossed in his booby trap.

"By the way, Carl, you ever met a guy named Simons?"

Mr Rood was startled enough not to answer instantly. He recalled his recent interviewer's emphasis on anonymity, and the advantage it offered to his own vanity which he had not overlooked in thinking about the proposition since, and decided that some professional reserve was justified.

"Why on earth do you ask that, Joseph?" he inquired cautiously.

"He's an attorney who's been bothering a friend of mine about some broad he may have knocked up," Sholto said. "I just thought you might know him."

"Oh, no," said Mr Rood, relieved that he was not to be faced with a problem. "I don't believe I know anyone of that name."

They signed off with the conventional cordialities, and Sholto slammed down the receiver and hurled his cigar stump savagely into the fireplace.

"The dirty, stinking, lying, double-crossing son of a bitch!"

His first lieutenant was already looking at him in full comprehension, but Sholto's indignation had to have the first outlet of words.

"If he hadn't told me before, that was his chance to say something. That's when he *had* to say it, if he was ever going to be on the level. But no. 'I don't believe I know anyone of that name,' he says. The bastard! I need to hear the rest of that tape like a hole in the head. I *know* what he must've said to Simons."

He pulled the spool of tape off the recorder and glowered at it for a moment as if he were wondering what insensate violence to inflict on it. Then he took out another cigar, bit off the end, lighted it, and went back to his armchair. He sat in hard-mouthed grim-jawed silence which his lieutenant was too wise to interrupt, turning the spool over and over monotonously in one hand; and there was something even more terrifying in his impassive concentration than in his rage.

It was an hour and a half before the telephone rang again, and he heard the voice of his henchman in Biloxi.

"I think I got all you wanted, Dibs."

"What is it?"

"The dame has a newsstand-shop here in town. Had it five years. She lives with a married sister. But right now she's away. She went to California to have her eyes operated on, account of she's blind. Seems someone met her in the shop and offered to pick up the tab, but nobody knows who he was. Nobody else saw him, and she couldn't tell anything about him, account of being blind. A mystery man."

"Do they know where she went in California?"

"Santa Barbara. I got the name of the doctor. I'll spell it out for you——"

Sholto wrote it down, grunted his thanks, and hung up. He took out another cigar, and this time he carefully cut off the end.

"That's all we need," he said, and repeated what his correspondent had told him.

"Didn't he get the address where she is?" asked the lieutenant.

"What's that matter?" Sholto snarled. "If the doc clams up, we ask all the hospitals. There can't be so many in Santa Barbara." He was not to know that the Saint had already foreseen and forestalled this. "Get that crummy pee eye back here."

Simon Templar entered with the air of thinly disguised

nervous expectancy proper to his part, and Sholto wasted no time crushing him.

"I thought your proposition over, bub, and it's no sale."

"You mean you don't *want* to know what Mr Rood said?"

"I know what he said. You ain't dumb enough to think you could get away with a record of him turning this guy Simons down, so I guess he says okay. I don't pay ten grand to hear that."

"But you'd like to find Mrs Yarrow, wouldn't you?"

"I'll find her if I want to, and cheaper than you can do it."

"But after all, Dibs," whined the Saint aggrievedly, "if I hadn't——"

"Yeah, I know," Sholto said. "I do owe you something for the tip-off. And nobody ever said I welshed on nothing reasonable. I don't have no obligation, but I'll pay you what I think the tape I heard is worth."

He dug into his pocket and pulled out a thick wad of green paper bound with a gold clip. He detached two bills from the top and held them out, and the Saint looked down and saw that the denominations were a thousand dollars each.

"Take it," Sholto rasped, "before I change my mind."

Simon swallowed and took it.

Then he turned to the second lieutenant, who had followed him back in, and produced a sheet from a score pad.

"And you owe me eighty-five dollars and ten cents, Earl," he said.

"Pay him," Sholto said. "And throw him out."

He stood at the window and watched the Saint's car going down the drive, and then turned briskly as the second lieutenant returned.

"Call the airport, Earl," he ordered. "Get us on the next plane to New York. We'll all go."

"What about the dame in California?" asked the first lieutenant.

"We'll have plenty of time for her. She's bound to be in the hospital for some time yet. But Rood won't wait. I could pass the word to the big boys, but I think we'll take care of him ourselves." Sholto took out the spool of tape and weighed it meditatively in his hand again. "I wouldn't be surprised to see 'em coming to us with their hats in their hands when they hear what I've done for 'em."

With no inkling of the rôle that had been chosen for him in Dibs Sholto's pursuit of his ambitions, Mr Carlton Rood returned to his apartment in the East Sixties that night after an excellent dinner, feeling very comfortably contented with the perspective of his life. His literary endeavour had been completed and safely deposited, and that very afternoon he had dropped the first strategically aimed word about it, in a quarter from which he knew the grapevine would rapidly circulate it to all interested ears. He felt a mild glow of gratitude to Mr Simons for the suggestion, and benevolently hoped that something good would come of the business they had discussed.

As he reached the doorway, two men got out of a car parked nearby and came quickly towards him. Mr Rood saw them out of the corner of his eye, and suddenly realized that what he had glimpsed of one of them was familiar. He turned, and recognized a valued client.

"Why, Joseph!" he exclaimed. "This is a surprise——"

"I bet it is, you lousy squealer," Sholto said, and personally fired the first shot of a fusillade.

"You see," said the Saint tranquilly, "the law of the land says that if there's any reasonable doubt about a man's guilt, he must be acquitted. The law of the underworld is just the opposite. On the other side of the fence, if there's any serious doubt about a man's reliability, they make sure he can't possibly worry them any more. I thought that since Carlton Rood had worked so hard to protect the tribe that lives by that philosophy, he might like to have it tried on himself."

"I'm sure he loved it," said his friend the ophthamologist. "But what about this sequel?"

He indicated the newspaper they had been looking at, which reported the finding of a body identified as that of Joseph ("Dibs") Sholto, fatally laden with lead, in a garbage dump somewhere in Jersey.

"When the notes that Rood left reached the Department of Justice and various district attorneys, and the heat started sizzling all over, the big boys naturally blamed Sholto for starting the whole thing. And out of his own bailiwick, too. So they had to teach him a permanent lesson. The ordinary dull due process of Law might have taken care of him anyway, with the help of Rood's contribution, but they saved it the trouble. I can't say I was so sure of that, but I was hoping for it. Let's call it a bonus."

"I'd be sorry for Machiavelli," said the doctor, "if the poor naïve man had ever come up against you."

Simon Templar grinned gently; and his friend glanced at his watch and stood up.

"If you can come to the nursing home now," he said, "Mrs Yarrow was most anxious that if we have succeeded, the first person she sees would be you...."